JINGLE BELLS AND WEDDING SPELLS

Mystic Inn Mysteries

Book 8

STEPHANIE DAMORE

Chapter 1

The lobby of Mystic Inn was warm and cozy with a crackling fire in the fireplace, garland strung across the mantel, and twinkling white lights reflecting off the gold candle holders. Aunt Thelma had magicked the air to smell perpetually like cinnamon, adding to the festive atmosphere and making me crave Diane's cinnamon rolls from her bakery, La Luna.

In the corner of the lobby was a beautiful twelve-foot spruce Christmas tree decorated with sparkling ornaments and multi-colored lights. Next to the tree, Aunt Thelma had set up a miniature Christmas village with tiny shops, evergreens, fake snow, and even a replica of Silverlake's famous witch fountain that stood at the center of Wishing Well Park.

On the side table, a tray of frosted sugar cookies

from La Luna was on display, inviting guests to indulge in a sweet treat as they passed. The warm glow of the fire and the festive decorations made the lobby feel like a magical winter wonderland.

I stood behind the front counter, checking in a group of guests. As I handed them their room keys, I couldn't help but feel excited about my upcoming wedding.

"Oh, I know that look," Aunt Thelma interrupted my daydream. I hadn't even realized she'd come out of the back office. "You're thinking about the big day, aren't you?" she asked with a smile.

"What? No." I shook my head as if the action added weight to my statement. "I was mentally calculating how many more guests still need to check in tonight."

"I don't know why you try to deny it. A bride is supposed to daydream about her wedding, especially when it's only days away. I don't know why you insist on working right up to it."

"Because if I didn't, I'd walk around with my head in the clouds all day, and where would that get me? No, I'd rather be busy here."

"If you say so, but I have to tell you, I stopped by the church, and the decorations are beautiful. Father George said the Christmas tree is over fifteen feet tall this year. The ladies guild went all out with the poinsettias at the altar and holly and candles on every window ledge. The way the candles light up the stained glass windows? Well, it's even more magical than I could've ever dreamed, and that's saying something."

At first, I wasn't sure about a winter wedding, but it didn't take me long to warm up to the idea. The beautiful church decor was the icing on the cake.

"Only five more days until the big day," I said. My voice hitched at the end from nerves.

Aunt Thelma smiled. "I know, dear. It's getting closer and closer, but don't worry. Clemmie and I have taken care of everything. It's going to be perfect."

"I'm sure it will be." I wasn't one to gush poetically, but I was excited to marry Vance. I couldn't wait to see the look on his face when I walked down the aisle in my custom-made gown. It was the one thing I'd picked out.

"You two are going to be so happy together," Aunt Thelma said.

I replied with a smile. After our twenty-year history together, it was finally time for us to be happy. I wasn't going to worry about anything, including the warning from Amelia, the young psychic, this past fall. My best friend Misty almost destroyed her relationship by taking the psychic's words to heart. I refused to do that. I wasn't going to worry about anything until I had a reason to, and so far, things were moving along without a hitch. It was time that I focused on the good and enjoyed the moment. I said as much to my aunt.

"That's the spirit," Aunt Thelma said, patting me on the back as another group of guests walked through the door.

I might've been excited about my upcoming wedding, but that wasn't what was driving the tourists into town tonight. No, tonight was the hot cocoa crawl at Village Square, followed by the tree-lighting ceremony at Wishing Well Park. The quaint outside shopping district was hosting the event. It was like Christmas trick-or-treating. You could go from shop to shop, trying different hot cocoas and toppings like candy canes, whipped cream, chocolate shavings, and sprinkles. Some shops were also giving out little gifts like bath bombs filled with calming potions courtesy of Connie at her potion shop, gourmet marshmallows from Luke at the candy shop, and buttered shortbread from Diane's bakery. Rumor had it the Tavern was also offering a variety of festive spirits to spike your brew. There was even a chance to win the grand prize, a magical getaway to Mount Holly. The Christmas Village celebrated Yuletide three hundred and sixty-five days a year and was known to bring out the Christmas spirit in the grinchiest of witches.

"You're not going to believe it, but I think it's going to snow tonight," Vance said when he entered the lobby a few minutes later. Aunt Thelma and I had been alone in the lobby once more. Vance brushed a few droplets off his black wool coat.

"Is it raining out?" I looked across the room and out the patio doors, but it was too dark outside to make out anything. I couldn't even see the lake. As much as I enjoyed the cheer of the holiday season, part of me missed the long summer nights, sipping glasses of wine on the patio and watching the swans glide across the water.

"A little bit. It's more like freezing rain at this point, but if the temp drops like they say it will, it'll turn to flakes in no time."

"Wouldn't that be a miracle?" Aunt Thelma chimed in. "Snow in Silverlake without using a spell." My aunt winked.

"Wait, you didn't cast a weather spell, did you?" Something about the mischievous twinkle in my aunt's eye made me not trust her.

"Wouldn't tell you if I did." Aunt Thelma smiled and disappeared into her back office.

"She's trouble; you know that?" I said to Vance with affection in my voice. Both she and her best friend, Clemmie; you had to watch it with those two.

Chapter 2

As we walked through Village Square, I was struck by the beauty of the holiday decorations. The district was awash with the warm glow of bright Christmas lights. The Town Council had wrapped strands of colorful bulbs around lampposts and draped them across storefronts, casting a festive atmosphere over the bustling sidewalk. The shops were dressed in their holiday finest with garlands of pine and holly adorning their windows and doors. A local artist had painted winter scenes on the front windows of some of the shops. The jeweler's large window displayed a carefully painted festive portrait of Santa Claus and his reindeer flying through a starry night sky.

As visitors bustled about, their breath misting in the cold air, the sounds of carolers filled the air. A group of rosy-cheeked singers stood on the corner, belting out traditional holiday tunes as they collected donations for a local charity.

Despite Vance's assurances that it was going to snow, the Town Council had taken no chances, choosing to blanket the rooftops in fluffy white cotton instead of using a weather spell. Snow and ice were beautiful, but they could be a hassle to deal with when it came to shoveling sidewalks and salting roads.

As we walked, we saw other people enjoying the hot cocoa crawl, going from shop to shop, and trying different flavors and toppings. The warm glow of the lights and the carols added to the joyous atmosphere. I couldn't help but feel excited, surrounded by the season's magic.

"Hey, guys, congrats on the upcoming wedding!" Elizabeth said as she passed by with Cassidy. Elizabeth used to live one town over in Harrisville but recently moved in with Cassidy, one of our town's healers and owner of the apothecary. Elizabeth said she didn't have a reason to stay in Harrisville anymore after her uncle passed away, and she was ready to embrace more of her witchy side. The good witchy side, that is. Her family had a dark past, and Elizabeth had been working to pay off the 'karmic debt' ever since. Her words, not mine. I rather liked Elizabeth and not only because she helped me break a tricky curse. Elizabeth was a good person whether she believed it or not.

Luckily, Cassidy agreed, and she said she could use a hand at her store. After a shaky start, word of Cassidy's remedies got around, and she quickly made a name for herself. The two made a great team.

"Thank you!" Vance and I said in unison as we passed by. We would've stopped and chatted, but the ladies seemed like they were on a mission.

After grabbing a cup of cocoa from La Luna, we decided to head over to the Candy Cauldron for a gourmet marshmallow and to check in with Sabrina and Beatrice. The mischievous twins had kept to their word and were busy experimenting with different truffle flavors for the wedding. I'd hoped giving them something to do would keep them out of trouble. So far, the plan seemed to be working.

"Hey, Angelica, we're so excited about your big day," Beatrice said when we walked in.

"Are you here to sample one of the truffles?" Sabrina added.

"Sure, if you have them ready."

"We might have one or two you can try," Sabrina said.

"But we can't give away the secret ingredient. You'll just have to trust us," Beatrice winked.

I glanced over at Vance. It was mighty hard to trust the twins. If you'd ever been on the receiving end of one of their pranks, you'd know why.

"GIRLS!" Luke's raised voice came from the kitchen. Their uncle poked his face out of the door, and I gasped. His entire face was covered in glitter like a disco ball. His eyes latched onto the girls. "Who switched out my wand for a trick wand?" he demanded.

The twins backed up, seeming to gauge how angry their uncle was. "Well, you did say tonight was a festive occasion," Beatrice started.

"And there's nothing more festive than glitter. Am I right?" Sabrina tried to smile.

"Girls." Luke's eye began to twitch, or maybe it was just reflecting off the overhead lighting.

"Sorry, Uncle Luke," Beatrice said, "but you have to admit it is pretty funny."

"And you look very festive!"

"And if we don't keep you on your toes, who will?" Beatrice added.

I shook my head. I looked over at the trouble-makers. "I thought you two had turned over a new leaf?"

"You can't expect us to be good all the time," Beatrice replied.

"We've been extra good lately, and it's exhausting," Sabrina replied dramatically.

Beatrice leaned in. "After this wedding business is over, all bets are off."

I looked over at Luke and wondered if he

wanted to ship his nieces off to boarding school now or wait until after the holidays.

Just then, their friend Amelia opened the door. "Hey, guys, are you coming to the hot cocoa crawl with me?"

"Of course," they said in unison.

"We wouldn't miss it for the world," Sabrina added.

"Nice glitter," Amelia added to Luke as the twins met up with her. The duo whisked their friend out the door before she could utter another word.

"Be back here by nine!" Luke hollered after them. Beatrice waved over her shoulder, indicating she'd heard him.

"Here, allow me." I withdrew my wand and pointed it at my friend's face. There was a time not too long ago when I was a walking disaster when it came to magic, but I'd since been practicing thanks to my tutor, Vanessa Ravenwood, headmistress of Mount Holly's School of Magic. I'd mastered a few mundane spells, such as conjuring wind or water, and Aunt Thelma promised to let me practice my defense magic against her later this week. I wasn't sure that was a smart idea, but she assured me she could handle it. But for now, I cleared my throat and said, "Anemos," in a clear and calm voice. A steady stream of pressurized air blasted Luke in his face as if I were wielding an air compressor and not a wand. The glitter blew around the candy shop like tiny silver snowflakes. Vance took a step back to make sure none landed on him.

I moved my wand around and tried to get all the remaining glitter off his face, but a few specks refused to budge. "I got most of it, but you might want to look in a mirror to get the rest."

"Those girls are going to be the death of me," he said with a sigh.

I hated to agree with Luke, but in this case, he may be right.

WE CAME to a stop outside one of Village Square's newer shops called The Charmery. The dazzling shop sold numerous types of charms for things such as love or luck. Even from the sidewalk, I could see the glimmer and sparkle of the shop's magical treasures. Like the other surrounding businesses, Honor had decorated her shop for Christmas with twinkling lights and festive garlands. A small Christmas tree stood in the front corner of the window, adorned with red ornaments, tinsel, and even more charms.

The Charmery's necklace display was unlike any I had seen before. Instead of being arranged on a counter or table, Honor hung them from delicate silver chains suspended from the ceiling. Each necklace was unique. Some were made of precious metals and gemstones, while Honor crafted others from seashells, feathers, or glass. I knew from stopping in before that each piece was labeled with a small tag indicating the type of magic the charm was infused with.

The soft overhead lighting showcased the beauty of each piece, and I felt drawn to explore the necklaces, which was surprising, seeing as I didn't wear much jewelry other than my sapphire engagement ring and tiger's eye pendant necklace. My necklace gave me, and me only, the ability to transform into a cat. Some people inherit fine china from their mother. I inherited transfiguration.

I peered through the window, spotting a charm in the shape of a circle about the size of a nickel in the front display. It looked like it was made of resin with flecks of gold and a coin suspended in the middle.

"That one's beautiful." I don't know why I pointed through the window. With so many charms, it was impossible for Vance to know which one I meant. "I wonder what it does?"

"Why don't we go inside and take a closer look?"

"Sure."

Vance opened the door, but as we entered the shop, we heard raised voices coming from the back. We froze. Vance and I silently gauged the situation as we walked the rest of the way inside. He closed the door softly behind us. I craned my neck to see if I could make out who was fighting and barely spotted Honor's bright blond hair. She was in the back hallway, facing us, but the majority of her body was blocked by the man standing toe to toe in front of her. I didn't recognize him from the back.

"You can't do this to me. You're the only one who can help me and you know it!" The man threw his arms up in frustration.

Vance and I exchanged a look. We didn't want to intrude, but we also didn't want to leave Honor alone. We took a few steps inside the store to get a better read of the situation.

The man continued shouting and waving his arms while Honor stood her ground, her face set in a determined expression. I still didn't recognize the man. I didn't think he was a local.

"I'm sorry, but I can't help you," she said firmly.

"You mean you won't."

Honor didn't reply.

"You'll regret this—mark my words. You'll regret it," the man snarled before storming out the back door, leaving Honor alone and visibly startled. She looked around the shop, her eyes wide and her hands shaking.

"Sorry about that," she said when she spotted us. She walked forward.

"Are you okay?" I approached her cautiously.

She looked up at us, her face pale and her

expression tense. She took a deep breath, trying to pull herself together.

"I'm fine. Thank you," she said, forcing a smile. "It was just a misunderstanding, nothing to worry about."

But Honor was shaken, and I couldn't help but wonder what caused the argument. Who was the man, and what did he want from her? I couldn't force her to tell me, and she clearly didn't want to talk about it.

As much as I wanted to pry, I didn't. Vance must've felt the same way as he directed Honor toward the window display.

I picked up his lead. "I spotted a charm in the window. It's beautiful. Can you tell me more about it?"

Honor followed behind me on autopilot. I could tell her mind was still arguing with the man who'd just stormed out. I didn't blame her, but after seeing the charm I meant, Honor seemed to relax, and a small smile appeared. "That's one of my favorite pieces." She walked over and picked up the charm. She held it up to the light. "It's a protection charm. It wards off bad luck and helps the wearer feel more confident and grounded. Personally, I love how it makes me feel safe and secure."

Honor removed a similar charm hidden on a gold chain tucked under the front of her shirt. "It's how I can stand up to customers like that," Honor motioned to the back of the shop, "without losing my cool."

I went to ask more about the altercation, seeing as Honor gave me an opening, but she cut me off. "No, don't worry about it. Honestly, it was nothing and not worth our energy. Now back to this charm. Do you want to try it on?"

I smiled. "I would love to."

Chapter 3

"Are you warm enough?" Vance asked as we continued to walk along the cobblestone path. Vance's prediction had come true, and it had started to snow. Either Mother Nature had gotten the Christmas memo, or Aunt Thelma hadn't taken any chances and created a fresh batch of winter weather.

"Mmm-hm." I was warm and toasty thanks to the protection charm sitting snuggly against my chest. The necklace was slightly longer than my tiger's eye pendant, allowing me to layer the two. My two magical amulets left me feeling safe and cozy. I didn't have time to say anything else as a snowball sailed over my head. From the massive mound of snow that had magically appeared at the center of Village Square, it was clear that someone had conjured the pile from somewhere remote like the North Pole, where no one would miss it.

A massive snowball fight erupted. Beatrice and Sabrina were ruthless with their aim, sending snowballs flying through the air with impressive speed and accuracy. Amelia was just as bad, laughing and dodging as she pelted anyone who came within range. I spotted my best friend, Misty, and her boyfriend, Daniel, diving into the action. They were braver than I was.

But the real surprise was Aunt Thelma, who was in on the snowball fight with Clemmie. The older ladies used their wands and magic to rapidly sail the snowballs through the air, hitting their targets with precision.

As the snowball fight raged around us, Vance and I ducked and ran for cover, but it was difficult to avoid the snowballs that flew past us, and we got pegged several times.

"I might be warm at the moment, but I'm not dressed for this," I said, shivering as a snowball hit me square in the chest.

"Me either." We continued to run, ducking and dodging as we went. Luckily, we spotted Connie, the potion master, standing outside her shop. She wore a Santa hat and a broad smile. Seeing us headed her way, she opened the door and ushered us inside.

"Come on in, you two, before you freeze to death," Connie said, laughing.

At first glance, Connie's shop always looked chaotic, but it was only because of how many potion ingredients and supplies she carried. The walls were lined with shelves filled with bottles and jars of shimmering liquid and dry ingredients. A golden cauldron bubbled and emitted a steady stream of steam from behind the counter.

"What are you brewing up tonight?" I asked, sniffing the air. The spicy aroma of cinnamon and nutmeg filled my senses, making me feel instantly at home.

Connie hurried over to the cauldron and stirred the shimmering liquid. "Hang on. You have to try this."

I looked skeptical. Connie was one powerful potion master. She could knock you out for hours, make you relive your worst memory, or have you quacking like a duck before you knew what hit you.

"I promise it's a harmless spell. You'll love it."

"It isn't going to make me relive my childhood or have weird dreams or something, is it?" I asked. Vance turned to Connie. He seemed to have the same question.

"Not this one. Trust me." Connie carefully ladled the steaming hot potion into two mugs and handed one to Vance and me. "Here, try it."

I sipped the potion hesitantly. A wave of warmth flowed through my body, and I felt a cozy, comforting feeling settle over me like a warm blanket fresh out of the dryer.

"Okay, that's impressive." My eyes were wide with amazement. I hadn't realized how cold my toes were until they grew warm and toasty. And here I thought my new charm had been keeping me warm.

"You could make a fortune off of this stuff," Vance remarked.

"Especially after that snowball fight wraps up." I motioned with my head out the front window.

"I hope so. With the price of potion ingredients going up, I could use it. Anyway, I'm glad you both like it. It's a special recipe I only bring out during the holidays. I make it with a dash of magic and a whole lot of love."

I took another sip of the potion, feeling its warmth spread throughout my body.

"So, how many more days until the big day?" Connie changed the subject.

"Five," I replied while Vance was mid-sip.

Connie looked up and off to the side as if she were doing math in her head. "That should give me enough time," she said to herself.

"Enough time for what?" I looked over at Vance to see if he knew what Connie was talking about.

"Oh, nothing. Forget I said anything."

I would have to because, at that moment, Aunt

Thelma and Clemmie burst into the shop. It turned out their magic was no match for the trio of relentless young witches. Aunt Thelma's strawberry blonde hair was damp with her side bangs plastered to her forehead. Clemmie wasn't taking any chances, and she locked the door behind her.

"Those girls are animals!" Clemmie said while laughing as she took in Aunt Thelma's disheveled appearance.

"I don't know what you're laughing at. You're every bit of a mess as I am."

"Ladies, come on over here. I'll have you set to right in no time," Connie instructed before turning to Vance. "Unlock the front door, will you? The girls know better than to mess with me."

Vance nodded. I was pretty sure everyone knew not to mess with Connie. You'd be a fool if you did.

"I only have one question. Who started it?" I asked Clemmie and Aunt Thelma while Connie ladled out two more mugs of her special holiday potion.

Both of the women pointed at one another. "She did!" they said in unison.

"Who said 'let's give those youngins a run for their money'?" Clemmie asked my aunt.

"I might have said that, but who threw the first snowball?" Aunt Thelma remarked while accepting a mug from Connie.

"After you conjured a mountain of snow from

the Himalayas." Clemmie accepted the second mug from Connie.

"And here I thought it was the North Pole," I interrupted.

"Oh no, you can't steal Santa's snow. That would never go over well," Aunt Thelma replied with all seriousness.

For not the first time, my aunt left me speechless.

"What time is it?" Clemmie asked, setting down her mug and looking at her wristwatch.

"Almost eight," Vance replied.

"Shoot. We better all get going if we're going to catch the tree lighting. Connie, thank you for the potion. One sip and I already feel toasty. Mind if I take it to go?" Clemmie was already heading to the door with the brew.

"You're all more than welcome to. Just bring the mugs back," Connie replied.

"Thank you, dear." Aunt Thelma closed the distance between her and Connie and gave her a one-armed hug. "Guess we better be off. Are you two lovebirds coming along?" My aunt turned to Vance and me.

"Shouldn't it be turtledoves?" Clemmie asked.

"Hmmm?" Aunt Thelma replied.

"Turtledoves, not lovebirds," Clemmie repeated.

"Why would I say turtledoves? That doesn't make any sense."

"'Cause it's Christmas, and you have the partridge in the pear tree and all that."

Aunt Thelma turned to Connie. "What potion did you give her?"

"Oh, never mind, let's get going," Clemmie said. The two ladies followed one another out the door. I could hear Clemmie say, "Don't you know the Twelve Days of Christmas song?'"

"I still don't know what that has to do with love-birds," Aunt Thelma quipped.

"I suppose we better follow along. Connie, thank you for the potion. It was impressive, as always. I've already finished mine, but I'll pass the word around."

"Same. I don't even feel like I need to wear a coat," Vance agreed.

"Thanks, guys, I appreciate it. Have fun out there."

THE CRISP WINTER air was alive with excitement as Mayor Parrish stood at the center of the park, surrounded by a crowd of eager townspeople. A giant Christmas tree loomed behind her, its branches bare and waiting.

Aunt Thelma and Clemmie saved us a spot right up front. Vance and I joined the duo.

"Can everybody hear me? Can everybody see me?" Mayor Parrish waved her gloved hand in the air to get everyone's attention while speaking into a microphone.

A round of cheers and applause greeted the mayor.

"Excellent." Mayor Parrish cleared her throat. "Welcome, everyone, to the annual tree lighting ceremony!" she exclaimed, her voice ringing out over the crowd. "Are you ready to bring some holiday cheer to Silverlake?"

The crowd cheered and clapped, and Mayor Parrish smiled brightly. She bent low, plugged one end of the extension cord into a nearby outlet, and then turned to the tree. The mayor bent down again and tried to plug the other end into the base of the tree, but to her surprise, there was not enough cord. She tugged at it, but it seemed to be caught on something.

"Oh no, what's happening?" Mayor Parrish muttered, frowning in confusion. "Hold on, everyone, I just need to untangle this." Mayor Parrish tried to keep her voice cheerful. The mayor tilted her head from side to side, trying to determine where the hang-up was.

"I think it's caught on the back of the tree," Aunt Thelma remarked at the same time I'd realized the same thing. I wasted no time heading around the back of the massive evergreen to help untangle the snag. Vance moved with me.

In the darkness, it took me a minute to make out what the cord was snagged on. I could see that something was off. The lights were tangled and disorderly, and there was a dark shape slumped against the base of the tree.

Vance and I exchanged a look of concern, and we hurried over to investigate. As we got closer, we realized with a start that it was a man, and he was clearly dead. His eyes were closed, and his skin was pale. A web of Christmas lights was tangled around his neck and arms.

"Gah!" I jumped back and crashed right into Vance's chest. He protectively wrapped his arms around my waist. My heart raced with shock.

Just then, Mayor Parrish came around the corner. "Did you straighten it all out?" Her cheery expression faltered once she took in the scene.

I swallowed hard, trying to find the words to explain our grim discovery. "Mayor Parrish...there's been a...a terrible accident."

Vance took over. "This man is dead, tangled in the Christmas lights. We need to call the police."

Mayor Parrish's smile faltered. "No, no, that can't be right. Tonight is supposed to be a night of celebration. We can't have a dead body. Who is it?" The mayor squinted into the darkness, seeming more concerned for the ruined lighting ceremony than the poor man's fate.

Vance recognized him before I did. Maybe that was because he was willing to get up close and take another look. "I don't know his name, but he's the guy we saw at The Charmery tonight."

I did a double-take.

"What's this now?" Mayor Parrish asked for clarification.

"Hang on before we recap everything. Is Deputy Jones here?" I'd rather talk to the male deputy than his counterpart Amber or her daddy, the sheriff. Amber had grown a lot over the last two years, but she still wasn't my law officer of choice.

"My word. You found another dead body?" Clemmie's words rang out across the park. I hadn't even realized Clemmie and my aunt had come around back.

"Dead body?" someone said from out front. In seconds, gasps and murmurs rippled through the crowd.

"Was that really necessary?" Mayor Parrish admonished Clemmie.

"Deputy Nightingale," Sheriff Reynolds met us around back.

I tried not to show my disappointment at his arrival, nor did I correct his use of my title. I technically was still a deputy from this past summer even if I didn't exercise any authority. Frankly, I was surprised the sheriff addressed me as such.

"What happened here?" he asked, his face grim but not as stern as usual.

"This man has ruined the town's Christmas lighting ceremony. That's what's happened," Mayor Parrish answered.

"Maybe you should go out front and say something," Sheriff Reynolds said, trying to get rid of the mayor.

"Me? What in heavens am I going to say? I don't want to be the face of bad news. That's political suicide."

"My word, I'll go do it. C'mon, Thelma." Clemmie motioned to my aunt to follow her.

I spoke up. "I'm not sure who this man even is, but Vance and I saw him arguing with Honor tonight at The Charmery." I couldn't help looking down at the deceased man. The strand of Christmas lights had been wrapped tightly around his neck, choking him. This was no accident. This was murder.

The sheriff nodded, taking out his notebook and pen. "I need you to tell me everything you saw and heard."

Vance and I took turns recalling as much information as we could. It wasn't much, but it at least gave the sheriff a lead. As we talked, Deputy Jones and Amber arrived on the scene and secured the area. Amber's boyfriend, Dippy, the ice cream man, stood off to the side, looking like he was about to toss his cookies. Death had a tendency to do that to some people. Yet, Dippy didn't seem able to leave Amber's side. I guess that was one definition of true love.

"I think that's about it," I said after we recapped the evening.

The sheriff closed his notebook. "Now, before I go tracking down Honor, is there anything else you're leaving out? Like you already know who the killer is, and you can save me some trouble?"

I laughed. "I swear. I have no clue."

"Didn't hurt to ask." I had to agree with the sheriff there. I might have been known to withhold information a time or two. "All right then, this is the part when I tell you to keep your nose out of my case."

"Don't worry. We have no plans on getting involved." I looked to Vance.

He nodded. "Our wedding's this weekend," he supplied to the sheriff.

"And I don't want anything to ruin it. Plus, this doesn't seem like a random murder. I can't believe Honor has anything to do with it, but she'll at least tell you who he is."

The sheriff nodded. "I'll be in touch. Let me know if you think of anything else, and congratulations on your upcoming nuptials."

Vance and I walked away from the crime scene. "Wow, is it just me or was Sheriff Reynolds actually nice to us?" I asked Vance.

"You should've saved his daughter's life a long time ago," Vance remarked, referencing the last case.

"Yeah, no doubt."

Chapter 4

The next morning, I sat at the kitchen table, picking at my breakfast as I thought about the previous night's events. I was still shaken by the discovery of the body behind the Christmas tree, and I couldn't release feeling guilty for not being able to help the sheriff more, which was ridiculous. I didn't have to jump in and solve every crime in Silverlake. I knew that, but I also couldn't stop thinking about Honor. I hoped she wasn't involved in the murder. She was relatively new in town, but from what I knew of her, she was very kind and sweet.

Suddenly, Aunt Thelma bustled in the front door. She had been downstairs working the front desk, so her appearance was a surprise. She was still talking on the phone when she said to me, "Did you hear the news?"

I shook my head, unsure of what my aunt was referring to. "What news?"

"Honor seems to have skipped town. The sheriff can't find her anywhere to question her about the murder."

My heart sank as I realized the implications of this news. If Honor were guilty of the murder, she likely fled to avoid being caught, and if she were innocent, she could be in danger from the real killer. Either way, she was tied to the murder. My sense of guilt only seemed to compound.

"Who is Honor friends with? Because she doesn't have any family in town, does she?"

"That's what Clemmie and I were just talking about. Clemmie says she's from Texas but hangs out with Pauline Ruble from time to time. They were just at her tea shop yesterday."

"Pauline, who works at the wand shop?"

Aunt Thelma relayed my question to Clemmie and waited for the response. "She says that's the one."

I nodded as I thought things through. It was Tuesday morning, and I didn't have to work until tonight. I almost always walked over to the bookshop on my days off and hung out with Misty. It was our thing. Depending on how busy the bookshop was, she'd either be free to head down to the wand shop, Sticks, with me, or she might know who else Honor was friends with.

"I don't know if she's going to investigate or not, but she's got that look in her eyes," my aunt replied to her friend. There was a time when she would've begged me to stay away from murder, but apparently, she'd rather have me stick my nose in a mystery than stress her out about the wedding. Part of me loved the fact that she was planning it all, but the other part struggled to let go of the reins, even if it was the only way Vance and I would ever tie the knot.

"Of course, I'll look into it if she doesn't. Where do you think she gets it from?"

I looked at my aunt and shook my head. Leave it to her to take up the case if I didn't. I stopped that train of thought right then and there. I don't know who my aunt was kidding. She was bound to get in trouble if she got involved. Clemmie too. Those ladies had the best intentions, but their plans rarely turned out. I'd never forgive myself if something bad happened to either of them.

"I'll pop over and ask Pauline a couple of questions. Just a couple. Hopefully, she's working," I interrupted my aunt.

"Oh, that's just wonderful. Clemmie, did you hear that? She's taking the case!"

I didn't bother correcting my aunt. I doubted she would listen anyway. Besides, the wedding was still a few days away, and I didn't have much to do anyway. Aunt Thelma was true to her word and had planned everything. All Vance and I had to do was show up at the church. It wouldn't hurt to do some groundwork for the sheriff and let him know what I found out.

IT TURNED out I was alone. Misty was eating breakfast with Daniel at the diner. She'd invited me to join them, and believe me, I was tempted. Vance's mom, Heather, owned the place, and she could cook, but I also knew Misty and Daniel didn't get to spend a ton of time together. Being a rockstar, he was often on the road, and I didn't want to intrude.

I entered the wand shop, taking in the sleek, modern design. The walls were lined with gleaming wand displays, each showcasing a different type of wand. The floor was polished to a mirror-like shine, and the lighting was dimmed to give it an air of elegance. Flatscreen televisions displayed beautiful men and women modeling the wands in action, casting spells and performing spell-binding duels. Magic never looked so glamorous.

In the center of the shop, a bubbly woman with bright pink hair stood behind a counter, talking to Mrs. Potts, my retired second-grade teacher.

"Welcome to Sticks!" Pauline chirped. "I'll be with you in a moment."

Mrs. Potts waved from beside her, and I replied in kind.

I walked around the wand shop while listening to Pauline's sales pitch. As far as I knew, my friend Peter still owned the shop, but I hadn't seen him in town for months. Last I heard, he was expanding the brand on the west coast. Peter's vision for Sticks was grand and the reason why he and Misty had broken up over a year ago. She was disappointed when they split, but that was before she reconnected with Daniel.

"A team of expert wand makers craft every wand by hand," Pauline explained. "They use only the finest materials and the most advanced magical charms to create the perfect wand."

Mrs. Potts looked hesitantly at the high-end display.

Pauline quickly pivoted. "If you don't need something quite so fancy, we also have a wide variety of pre-made wands. They have less personalization but all the same power."

Mrs. Potts twisted her lips. "That might be more up my alley."

Pauline walked closer to me and plucked a wand out of the nearby display. The wand had floated effortlessly in the shadow box.

"How about the Luna Wand? It's our most popular design." Mrs. Potts took the wand from Pauline. "This one is made from a single piece of silver wood and is incredibly powerful. It's also incredibly rare, so we don't have many in stock, but it's worth it for those lucky enough to get their hands on one."

Mrs. Potts tested the weight in her hand and then held the slim piece of wood up to her spectacles to examine it. "I don't know. It sounds expensive."

"I like to think of it as an investment." Pauline beamed.

I caught Mrs. Potts' eye and smiled.

"Excuse me, won't you?" Mrs. Potts patted Pauline on her arm and walked over to me. Pauline stepped aside but kept an ear out.

"What do you think about all these fancy wands?" Mrs. Potts kept her voice low.

"Peter customized one for me a while back. I love it, but it wasn't cheap."

"I don't mind spending the coin as long as the quality's there."

"If Peter's name is still attached to the store, you can guarantee it is."

"Peter still oversees everything," Pauline chimed in before she could help herself. I eyed the somewhat pushy woman. "I'm sorry. I'll leave you two to it."

"I was going to say that if you're not in a rush, why not take some time to think about it?"

"I do need a new wand, but it's not an emergency." Mrs. Potts seemed to think about it some more. "Perhaps I'll have a cup of tea with Clemmie and think it over."

"I think that's a wonderful idea." I hated being pushed into buying something before I was ready. I didn't want Mrs. Potts to feel the same way.

"Thank you, dear. Perhaps you could come over for tea sometime?"

"I would love that."

"After the wedding?"

"That would probably be best."

Mrs. Potts squeezed my hand and left the store.

Pauline wasted no time approaching me. Mrs. Potts wasn't even all the way out the door before the bubbly woman said, "Thanks for your help back there." She then lowered her voice. "I heard you say how much you enjoy your Sticks wand. Honestly, I really do think they are the best, or else I wouldn't be able to look at myself in the mirror every morning."

I nodded to accept the compliment even though I didn't feel like I had helped Pauline. It was more like I bought Mrs. Potts some time to consider the purchase.

"I hate working on commission," Pauline grumbled before perking back up as soon as she noticed I was watching. "So, what can I do for you today? Does your wand need repair? Or are you looking to upgrade? Peter created a new spell charm that adds an extra layer of protection. It's an identity charm. Once you activate it, no one else can use your wand. It's a free gift for all new purchases, or you can add it to your existing wand."

I blinked, taking in everything Pauline had just said. An identity charm wasn't a bad idea, but I'd have to come back for that later. I squared my shoulders and hoped to refocus the witch. "Actually, I came down here to talk to you about Honor."

Panic flashed in Pauline's eyes. "Honor?" the woman's voice wobbled. She turned and walked away from me and headed toward the front counter. I followed close behind. "I'm afraid I'm not much help. I haven't seen her lately."

It took every ounce of self-control not to call Pauline out. You didn't have to be psychic to know she was lying. Not only did the woman's voice shake, but she refused to make eye contact as she busied herself tidying up papers behind the already clean workspace.

I pressed on. "I was in her shop last night when a man argued with her. It's the same man who was murdered last night." Pauline shook her head as if willing me to quit talking, yet her lips remained closed. "I only want to make sure she's okay." I searched out Pauline's eyes until she was forced to look at me. Fear stared back at me from their green depths. I let the silence stretch between us.

Pauline looked away. When she glanced back,

her resolve was locked in place. "That's very nice of you, but I can't help you." She shrugged.

Then, out of the corner of my eye, I saw something small and brown scurry across the shiny polished floor. It darted from behind a back counter and disappeared down the hallway toward the bathrooms. My cat instincts went on red alert, and my nose began to twitch as my feline alter ego attempted to sniff out the mouse. Even though I hadn't gotten a clear look at it, I was almost positive that's what it was.

"You have a mouse." I started to move toward where the small animal had disappeared. Pauline grabbed me by the sleeve of my puffy coat, stopping me.

"I'm sorry, you must be mistaken. We don't have a mouse." Pauline didn't let go of my coat.

I took a step back so she was no longer tugging on the material. "I'm pretty good at sniffing these things out, and I'm almost positive it's a mouse."

"I'm sure it's fine." Pauline casually glanced down the hall. She let go of me only when she was sure the animal was gone. "And whatever it was, it seems to be gone now." She chuckled nervously. "And come to think of it, I haven't taken my morning break yet." Pauline ushered me toward the door. "If you don't need a wand or anything, I'll have to ask you to leave so I can lock up and step out for a few minutes."

"Oh, no problem. Mind if I walk with you?"

Pauline shook her head so fast it was almost like a nervous tick. "What? No, I'm not leaving. I meant I just wanted a couple of minutes to eat a snack I brought in peace, but thank you for the offer," Pauline quickly added.

I smiled politely, but I knew something was definitely going on here. Pauline was hiding something. I was sure of it.

Chapter 5

I left Pauline and headed to Diane's bakery to grab a cup of coffee for myself and Vance. I checked my watch. I knew he had court this morning, but he should be out by now, and I figured he could use a midmorning pick-me-up. Besides, I wanted to share Pauline's behavior with him. As much as I wanted to know what she was hiding, it wouldn't do me any good to sit outside her shop and watch her all day. I would have to be more creative than that, and it might involve me transforming into my fluffy alter ego, Penelope, and sneaking back into the shop. Misty had given my cat the nickname. It was much easier to blame shenanigans on Penelope. Speaking of which, maybe Clemmie would be down for a bit of recon work later. I didn't want my aunt and her going off alone and sleuthing, but I'd take Clemmie as a sidekick. She was always good at creating a distraction.

Diane wasn't at the bakery, which meant I was in and out with two cups of coffee in record time. I only briefly stopped to say hello to Molly McCormick. We'd been friends in high school and still chatted from time to time, but mostly when I stopped by the bank where she worked. I owed Molly my life after I'd been held at gunpoint one time, and she witnessed the abduction on the bank's security system. I really hated it when people pointed guns at me.

Vance's office was on the other side of town in the business district where the courthouse, sheriff's department, and a handful of other businesses like the bank, post office, and library were located. It was also the location of the church Vance and I were getting married at.

I drove from our side of the lake to the business district, passing by the campground as I did so. One of the things that I loved about living in the lake community was how peaceful it was. The lake always seemed to calm me, as did the surrounding forest. Silverlake was a wonderful place to live. Everything was welcoming in the magical community from the quaint shops, to the perfectly manicured lawn of Wishing Well Park, the expansive surrounding forest, and the charming downtown area. Vance and I loved spending time outside.

Silverlake had plenty of hiking trails. Perhaps our most famous was the Enchanted Trail, which was a footpath that wound its way around the lake, but we also had others that snaked through the forest and opened to beautiful, picture-perfect meadows. Those magical spots were reserved for locals in the know and were the perfect place for a picnic. I thought maybe Vance and I could take a walk through the woods to help clear our heads ahead of the wedding. I felt it could do us some good, especially after the stress of finding the dead body last night.

As the church came into view, my mind drifted back to the upcoming wedding. Vance and I trusted Aunt Thelma with planning every aspect of the wedding, which meant a lot of it was a surprise. It sounded like a great idea at the time because we hadn't had any time to plan anything, but now my Type A personality was having a hard time not overseeing everything. This was my wedding we were talking about, and while the most important thing was that Vance and I were going to be married, I was anxious to see how everything was coming together.

All that explains why my car seemed to pull into the church's parking lot on autopilot. I quickly parked and jogged up the front steps.

As I approached the church, I caught sight of Rocky, one of the gargoyles perched atop the bell tower. The weathered stone figure was carved in the likeness of a fierce canine. He was stocky like a bulldog, with jowls to match. He had large, powerful wings, a sharp, toothy grin, and a tail like a devil. Despite his intimidating appearance, he was currently fast asleep, seemingly content to guard the church from his perch. I knew that Rocky only woke when danger threatened the town of Silverlake, and the rest of the time he was as solid as a rock. I couldn't help but feel a sense of comfort in his presence as I made my way up the front steps of the church. With one last wave to Rocky, I pushed open the heavy wooden doors and stepped inside, eager to take in the festive holiday decorations and visualize the wedding.

Aunt Thelma had been right. The church was truly magical. The three-storied building always seemed imposing with its grand bell tower and twin gargoyles perched on the ledge, but now, the building was decorated with all the trappings of the holiday. Wreaths of holly and evergreen adorned the doors and stained glass windows. Inside, the altar was decked out with a towering Christmas tree, its branches laden with sparkling ornaments and twinkling lights. The ladies' guild had arranged vibrant red poinsettias in festive gold pots along the altar. The air seemed to sparkle as if dusted with glitter. The guild had also fastened red and green ribbon to the end of the pews, and the air was filled with the warm, spicy scent of cinnamon and pine.

"Hello?" I called out as I walked up the aisle. My voice echoed throughout the sanctuary. I took a deep breath, allowing the peace of the space to wash over me. I wasn't surprised to find myself all alone. It was a weekday, and while Father George was often on site, he wasn't here all day long. However, the church sanctuary was open twenty-four-seven but just the sanctuary. The adjoining fellowship hall and office were closed unless it was during service or special events.

I took a couple more deep breaths once I reached the front of the church and turned to face the congregation, imagining what the view would look like this weekend.

Butterflies danced in my stomach, and I felt giddy with anticipation. Our wedding was decades in the making, and I couldn't believe it was finally here. Or it would be within a few days. Coming home had turned out to be the best decision of my life. It truly went to show you that you don't always know best. I thought I'd never return to Silverlake; that there was nothing left for me here, but it turned out that even without my relationship with Vance, Silverlake was where I belonged. Our love was a bonus.

After another look around, I made my way back down the aisle and headed outside to the real world.

The church's heavy wooden door had barely closed behind me when a sonic boom blasted from inside the church. The explosion was sudden and intense. The sound was deafening like a thunderclap that seemed to shake the very ground beneath my feet. The blast wave hit me like a physical force, throwing me forward and off balance. I fell onto the cement, covering my head with my hands. The weight of something heavy landed on top of my back. The air whooshed out of my lungs at the unexpected force, pining me in place. It took me a moment to realize the presence was protecting me.

The weight of something heavy lifted off my back, and a soft nudge on my face brought me back to consciousness. It was Rocky, one of the church's gargoyles. He was checking on me, making sure I was okay. I looked around and saw that the church was in ruins, debris scattered all over the ground. Glass littered the ground, and I looked up and spotted the second gargoyle circling above, as if on patrol for the cause of the blast.

Rocky licked my face, a sign that he was relieved that I was okay. I was a little shaky, but I managed to stand up. He nudged me forward, urging me to keep moving. I made my way down the remaining steps, and Rocky followed close behind, still checking on me. I took a quick inventory, and thankfully, I didn't seem to have any significant injuries. My puffy winter coat and mittens had kept me from getting cut by the glass, which fell out of my hair as I walked. I was grateful for Rocky's protection and comfort. He was more than just a stone statue, he was a protector, and in that moment, I needed him more than ever.

Being so close to the sheriff's department and city hall meant that in a matter of seconds, Sheriff Reynolds was on the scene with his entire task force. Our fire department and an ambulance quickly followed him. Both had automatically been dispatched onto the scene. I was okay, but a couple of other residents weren't quite as lucky. Poor Mr. McCormick. He was my friend Molly's dad and a Town Council member. It looked like he had been walking down the sidewalk when the blast occurred. He must've jumped back and tripped over the curb, falling backward and twisting his back. Mrs. White, our town librarian, had also fallen and now clutched her knee.

Fire Chief Grady approached me first as I was closest to the church, and asked if I was okay. I nodded mutely as I continued walking the rest of the way to my car, where I planned to sit until I could get my bearings. Rocky then nuzzled my hand with his snout as if to reassure me that I was indeed safe. I reached up and petted Rocky, grateful for his protection.

Rocky stayed by my side, his massive form towering over me as he stood protectively. I was alert enough to recognize I was in shock, as did Vance the moment he laid his eyes on me. I hadn't even made it back to my car. In three long strides, Vance ate up the distance between us

He instantly wrapped me in his arms and pulled me tightly to his chest, not caring that I had shards of glass stuck in my hair. He kissed the top of my head. I could feel his heart hammer madly in his chest, and it was then, when I knew that I was safe, that the tears began to leak out of my eyes.

Vance pulled back. "Let's get someone to look at you, okay?"

I nodded, still unable to find my voice.

Rocky, knowing that I was in good hands, took off to the skies, circling above the church to join his partner.

A few moments later, Aunt Thelma and Clemmie made an impressive entrance, zooming into the parking lot in Clemmie's brand-new black Cadillac. The ladies jumped out of the car as if they were superheroes ready to take down the villain, and not a couple of senior citizens, but the moment they saw me, their plans changed.

Cassidy, the town's healer, was fixing me up. I hadn't realized I'd scraped my face when falling to the ground, and my neck was also pretty stiff from being thrown forward. Thankfully, it was nothing she couldn't patch up in short order. She even knew a charm to make my ears stop ringing. Unfortunately, Mr. McCormick and Mrs. White needed a little more care, and they were whisked off to the community hospital.

"Are you okay, dear?" Aunt Thelma asked.

"What in the world happened here?" Clemmie inquired at the same time.

"Can't you see that the church exploded?" Aunt Thelma motioned to the stone building. The church's doors hung off their hinges, and the wreath was thrown to the ground.

"I can see that the church exploded. I want to know how our girl almost went ka-boom with it."

I winced.

Just then, Sheriff Reynolds and Fire Chief Grady arrived. I was sitting in the back seat of my car with the door open and my feet resting on the parking lot, giving Cassidy's charms another moment to finish healing me when they approached. I stood to greet them.

"Deputy Nightingale, glad you're all right," the sheriff said by way of greeting. I was beginning to realize the sheriff wasn't going to drop the 'deputy' moniker anytime soon. Knowing the sheriff, it had something to do with respect, and I'd earned it.

"Thanks." My voice sounded scratchy. I took a moment to clear my throat.

"You want me to go grab you a water?" Vance asked.

"There's a coffee for each of us in the front

seat." They were just out of reach to me. "Do you mind getting it for me?" Vance gave a curt nod, opened the passenger-side front door, and did just that.

"Do you mind telling us what happened?" Chief Grady asked while I took a sip.

"There's not much to tell. I stopped in the church to see how everything was coming ahead of the wedding this weekend." I turned to my aunt. "It was beautiful, by the way." I had no idea where we were going to get married now. Witches could be creative, but I doubted even my aunt could restore the church in a couple of days. I couldn't think about that right now, or I'd turn into an emotional mess. I turned back to the fire chief. "It happened right after I walked out of the church. The door closed behind me, and the next thing I knew, I was thrown to the ground."

"Does anything else jump out at you? Did something smell off inside the church, or did you hear any hissing noises?" the Fire Chief probed. I knew what he was getting at, but no, there was no evidence of a gas leak. I said as much.

"What do you think happened?" my aunt asked the fire chief.

"It's hard to say by looks alone. We're going to need to do a full investigation here." The fire chief looked to Sheriff Reynolds. He nodded in agreement.

"If you didn't want to get married, you could've just called off your wedding instead of blowing up the church."

I hadn't even seen Deputy Amber standing behind her father. I was about to shoot off a reproach, but her dad beat me to it.

"One would think you'd be more respectful to Deputy Nightengale after she saved your life, hm?" The sheriff raised his eyebrows at his daughter. His tone brokered no argument. The sheriff waited expectantly.

"You're right. I'm sorry, Angelica. Old habits die hard, I suppose."

I nodded to accept the apology and then wished I hadn't. Cassidy's tonic had taken the edge off my stiff neck, but it would still be smart to avoid sudden movements. The sheriff turned and began instructing his deputies where to begin. The group started coordinating their investigation with the fire chief.

"Hang on. I'll be back in just a minute." Vance touched my shoulder before walking off to meet Deputy Jones. The man, by far, was my favorite deputy. I always wished he'd run for sheriff, but even I had to admit that Sheriff Reynolds was growing on me. Things had definitely changed over the last couple of years in ways even I couldn't imagine.

I looked back at the church again, and my heart broke. My aunt read my expression.

"Now, don't you worry, dear. Clemmie and I will figure everything out. We'll find a new venue even more perfect than the church."

"Mm-hm, we sure will." Clemmie nodded.

"In fact, I have some ideas percolating in my head already. You free right now, Clemmie?"

"I sure am."

I tried to smile at the two women, but my heart wasn't in it. Aunt Thelma stepped forward and wrapped me in a hug. "Don't fret. I'll take care of everything. I promise," my aunt whispered in my ear. She pulled back.

"Thank you, both of you," I said to the ladies.

Vance rejoined us then.

"Everything okay?" I asked.

"Yeah, we're free to go. Are you sure you don't want to go to the hospital?" Vance asked.

"No, I'm fine. Feeling better by the minute. What did you find out? You have that look about you," I confessed.

"She's right. You do," Clemmie agreed.

Vance hesitated. He didn't hold out long with three women staring at him, waiting for answers. "We have a name on the victim from last night. I'd planned on calling Deputy Jones after court and seeing if you wanted to look into it, but that was before all of this," Vance confessed.

"I think that's a great idea," Aunt Thelma exclaimed.

"You do?" Vance and I said in unison.

"I told you so this morning. You're good at what you do. And with this explosion now? The sheriff isn't going to have time to hunt down a killer too. Our force is impressive, but there are only so many man-hours. Go, give them a hand. You are a deputy still, after all."

I had to admit that I did like solving mysteries. Surviving an explosion didn't change that, and just like I thought earlier today, it would be a good distraction.

"I think she's right." I turned to Vance.

He searched out my expression. "If only you're certain you shouldn't rest."

"I'm positive. I'm too keyed up now to rest."

"Okay, how about we head to the office?" Vance suggested.

"And we'll be at Clemmie's, planning the most beautiful wedding you could ever imagine. I guarantee it." I wasn't sure my aunt could pull that off with time running out, but I was willing to let her try.

Chapter 6

Seeing Vance had run over from the courthouse to the church, I decided to have him drive my car the short distance to his office. I know I had said I was feeling fine, but my hands were still a little shaky, and I wanted to give myself a minute to calm down before jumping behind the wheel. Vance didn't say a word as he slid behind the wheel and drove to his office; well, not about me anyway. "His name was Brent Cavalier. Deputy Jones said he had his driver's license in his wallet with a local Harrisville address."

Harrisville was one town over. It wasn't a magical town, but their former mayor had been a witch. Mayor Blackwell was the worst type of human being, and if you remember, all of his past deeds came back to haunt him one Halloween night not long ago. Other than Mayor Blackwell and his niece Elizabeth, I didn't know anyone from

Harrisville. Vance and I would go to dinner there from time to time, or we'd head that way if we needed something from one of the big box electronic stores, and it wasn't available to conjure from Witch-Mart, but that was it. "I'm hoping his address won't be too hard to track down. If not, Deputy Jones said he would call me back from his desk and relay the information."

"Did he say anything about a connection to Honor?"

"No, but I didn't even get a chance to ask him."

"That reminds me. I stopped by Sticks to talk to Honor's friend Pauline this morning." I went on to fill Vance in on my earlier conversation with Aunt Thelma and my plan to investigate a little bit ahead of the church explosion. I told him how Pauline had been eager to make a sale until I pointed out a mouse in the store, and she practically kicked me out.

"A mouse?" Vance looked over at me before keeping his eyes on the road and navigating into the parking spot in front of his office.

"I think it was a mouse. I suppose it could have been a hamster or maybe even a chipmunk." I shrugged. "It was something small and furry. Whatever it was, she didn't want me to go after it."

"Maybe she's scared of them?"

"You know, I hadn't thought about that." In a way, that would make sense. Maybe Pauline wanted to pretend that the mouse didn't exist because the truth was too upsetting.

"Not everyone thinks mice are cute and cuddly."

"And I feel sorry for them because mice are adorable; so are hamsters and guinea pigs. You know what? If an animal has fur, I think it's cute." Vance seemed to weigh his response before agreeing with me. "Anyway, even before the whole mouse incident, Pauline clearly did not want to talk about Honor, which means —"

"She knows something," Vance finished my sentence.

"Exactly."

"We're going to want to follow up with her or have the sheriff pay her a visit."

"I don't think she's going to tell them anything. I was thinking more of sneaking in as Penelope." Cats could uncover a lot.

"That's not a bad idea. Does she know you can transform?"

"I don't think so." Most people in Silverlake didn't know about my hidden talent unless they were long-time residents and were close to me, and Pauline was neither. "I was going to see if Clemmie wanted to go with me, but she's probably busy with my aunt now." My voice dropped at the end.

"Hey, look at me." Vance had parked the car, and we were ready to get out. "We don't have to get married right now. If you want to wait until the church is fixed, I'm more than happy to. I'm not going anywhere."

I met Vance's soulful expression. "I don't want to wait. I was really looking forward to this weekend, but I'm not sure Aunt Thelma will be able to pull it off." If I jumped in and tried to take the planning over, it would become the most stressful event of my life and not exactly how I wanted to remember our wedding day.

"How about we give them a day or two to see what they come up with, and if it's not what you want, we postpone everything until we can get it all sorted out?"

"Or we can go down to the courthouse and get married?" I asked hopefully.

"Or we go to the courthouse and get married. As long as someday you become my wife, I don't care about the when or the where."

"I feel the same way." Vance leaned in and met me across the center console of my car and gave me the sweetest, most reassuring kiss of my life. No matter what was happening in the outside world, I knew with him by my side, everything would turn out all right. Feeling lighter than I had five minutes ago, I stepped out of the car, ready to solve a mystery.

IT DIDN'T TAKE LONG for Vance to have Brent's Harrisville address. "What do you say we drive over to his house and check the place out? It looks like it's out in the country a bit." That was usually a good thing when it came to snooping around people's property. "Then, depending on what we find, we can either call the sheriff or stop and get a bite to eat. How does that sound?"

"I like it, except I want to stop by Honor's house first and make sure she isn't there. You know how the town gossip isn't always the most reliable." In fact, I should've started there this morning. Oh well, better late than never.

Vance agreed that it was smart to stop by Honor's and then we could take the drive out to Brent's.

We left my car, or rather the car that I shared with Aunt Thelma, at Vance's office and took his truck the short distance to Honor's duplex. There were some benefits to being a deputy after all, even if it was on a case-by-case basis, like obtaining people's addresses.

"I thought you were keeping out of it," Sheriff Reynolds said when I called for Honor's address.

"You and I both know I'm horrible at keeping my nose out of things." The sheriff grunted. "I'll call you and let you know what I find out." He grunted again. I assumed that meant I had his blessings.

The duplex was located on a quiet street near the high school. The neighborhood was average with a mix of single-family homes and small apartment buildings. The duplex itself was a two-story building with a small front yard and a driveway on one side. The exterior was a light gray color, and the windows were framed with white trim. The roof was black shingle, and the gutters were made of metal. The front door was a plain white wooden door with a small window on the top.

As we walked up the driveway, I could see that the duplex was well-maintained with a neatly trimmed lawn and a few bushes in the front yard with twinkling lights. The windows were clean and had white lace curtains hanging in them. The front porch had a small table, two chairs, and a potted mini-Christmas tree placed on the steps. A wind chime made of various charms hanging from the hook in the corner of the porch blew in the breeze.

I didn't waste any time and knocked quickly on the door.

Silence greeted us.

I tried again, this time adding a greeting, "Hello, Honor? It's Angelica. Are you home?"

Again, there was no response.

I took a step back and looked through the living room's front window. The window's sheer curtains were parted in the middle. The inside was cozy and homey. The living room was decorated with a mix of modern and vintage furniture. The walls were painted a pale blue color and had a few paintings and family photos hanging on them, but that was all I could see without looking too suspicious.

Behind us, the school was getting out for the day. Being a small community, all of the schools were stacked one right after the other. A mixture of school buses, parents, and teen drivers drove up and down the street, clogging the road and making it difficult to sneak around.

"I think this calls for a special appearance," I remarked.

Vance knew exactly what I was talking about.

"Do you want me to head to the car and keep a lookout?"

I eyed the pine tree at the corner of the house. It was just big enough for me to quickly duck behind and morph into Penelope. "Yeah, this should just take a minute."

I slipped behind the tree where hopefully no one was watching. Holding on to the tiger stone around my neck, I closed my eyes and said the incantation that would transform me into my feline alter ego: Metamorfóno alithís ousía.

As I cast the spell, I felt a warm sensation starting from the pit of my stomach that spread throughout my body. It started as a tingling sensation like pins and needles, and then grew into a feeling of warmth and energy. I felt as if I were being pulled and stretched in different directions all at once; as if my body were reshaping itself in an instant. The sensation was disorienting and dizzying, but it was also exhilarating. I felt the power of the spell coursing through my veins, and the energy of the transformation was almost electric. It was over in the blink of an eye.

I wasted no time scurrying along the back of the house to look in the window. Honor had a small backyard that looked exactly the same as her neighbors. Row after row, lot after lot, of squared-off backyards greeted me. The only thing that was different was there was a fence every now and then or a playset. I walked around to the cement slab back porch and looked into the sliding glass door. The only bad thing about being a cat was that I was looking at everything from a foot off the ground. I saw there was an old charcoal grill off to the side. I crouched low before springing up to land on top of the domed lid and get a better view of the house.

The kitchen was small but functional with white cabinets, and the walls were painted the same pale blue color as the living room, but it was the kitchen table that caught my eye. The kitchen was in order, but there was an unfinished cup of coffee on the kitchen table. Honor's journal was left open beside it, the open pen still sprawled across the page. A half-eaten muffin completed the scene.

I eyed the overhang on the porch before taking a

deep breath and making a jump for it. My front paws latched onto the shingles, and I was able to pull myself up until I was at eye level with the second story. I walked along the roof's edge. The space was about a foot wide. Shingles were on one side, and the gutter was on the other. I stopped when I reached the first bedroom. This one must've been a guest bedroom. The room was simple with a twin-size bed and a dresser, but that was all. It was sparse, to say the least. The second bedroom had to be Honor's. She'd pulled her clothes out of drawers and thrown half on the bed as if she'd been in a rush to pack. One suitcase was still left half-packed in the center of the room. I guess that answered that question. Honor had, in fact, run away, or someone had kidnapped her before she had the chance.

Chapter 7

It turns out that surviving an explosion and transforming into a cat in the same afternoon can take a lot out of you. After relaying the scene to Vance, I buckled up and prepared for the forty-minute drive to Harrisville. I'd like to say we had a deep and meaningful conversation on the ride across town or hashed out a theory for Honor's disappearance, but the truth was, being in Vance's presence soothed me, and I fell asleep before we even drove over Silverlake's covered bridge. I snoozed the entire way to Brent's property until Vance slowed down on the dirt road. The jostling ride shook me awake despite Vance's slow speed.

"Sorry, the road is pretty uneven," Vance apologized.

"That's okay." I stretched and yawned. My neck was still stiff but not too bad.

Vance slowed down to read the address off the rusty metal mailbox on the side of the road. "It should be one more."

I eyed the next property and could make out a ranch-style house set back from the road. Vance turned down the winding driveway. The main structure had a simple design with a sloping roof and large windows that let in plenty of natural light. The detached garage sat to the left of the house with two stalls with separate doors, and the outbuilding was to the right. On the side of the outbuilding was a large tractor with an old car next to it, rusting in the yard. Chickens seemed to come out of nowhere as we parked. They bobbed their heads, and I really hoped they weren't planning on chasing us. I know chickens are usually harmless, but every now and then, I've come across one who thought they were a raptor and gave me a run for the money.

We walked up the crushed stone driveway and headed toward the house.

I heard the shotgun ratchet before the man spoke. Vance had already grabbed my hand and was ready to bolt and get me to safety while I yanked my wand out of my pocket, ready to cast a defense charm.

"What are y'all doing here?" Something about the man's voice reminded me of a cowboy in an old western movie. We screeched to a halt and searched for the source of the voice. Hopefully, it was a good sign that the man had asked a question instead of shooting first.

Vance took the lead. "Excuse me, sir, but we're here for Brent Cavalier."

"He's dead."

I glanced up and saw the man for the first time. He had been working on another car in the garage when we approached. The cowboy image wasn't too far off the mark. The older man wore a black cowboy hat, and he had a shotgun down at his side. A toothpick poked out from between his lips.

"We know he's dead. What we meant was that we wanted to ask a few questions about him," I clarified.

"'Fraid I can't help you much."

I glanced down at the wand in my hand. I could make the man answer my questions, but that wasn't my style.

"What's that in your hand?" The man must've followed my eyes. "Is that a wand? Oh, cripes, it is. Don't tell me you're one of those hoodoo voodoo friends of his." The man shook his head. "I called Donovan and told him to come out here and clear out his brother's crap, but high and mighty hasn't made it out yet. Maybe you can take care of it. I want my workshop back." The man turned and motioned for us to follow him.

Vance and I looked at one another, trying to

keep up with the change in conversation and wondering what exactly the man wanted us to take care of. He stopped next to the second garage door and bent low to roll the square door up.

My eyes blinked to take the darkened space in. Vance and I stepped closer. The room was dimly lit and filled with magical objects. I could sense it. It made my skin crawl. I didn't know what kind of magic Brent was into, but I didn't like it. Shelves lined with ancient books and scrolls lined the walls. A foreign symbol had been painted in black onto the floor. The air was thick with the faint scent of burning candles and incense.

In the center of the room, there was a large wooden worktable cluttered with tools, including a set of balances, a mortar and pestle, and a variety of beakers and flasks. The tools were made of brass, iron, and other metals, and some of them looked like they were taken from an old laboratory. On the table, there were also some strange ingredients that you wouldn't find in an ordinary kitchen like small animal bones, herbs, and crystals of different colors.

"I would've never let him use the space if I'd known he was going to turn it into all this," the older man continued.

"I don't have the space for all of this, but I can call the sheriff. He's a friend of mine. He can stop by and take a look. He might be able to help clear it up," I offered, taking out my phone and snapping pictures of the space.

I wasn't sure how the man would react to my sheriff comment, but he surprised me when he replied with a nod. "'Suppose that would be all right. I just want it out of here."

"What was your name again?" I asked as politely as possible.

"Dwayne Robinson. This here is my property." The man went back to chewing on his toothpick.

"Was Brent staying here long?" Vance asked.

"Ever since his divorce. Thought it would be for a few months, but here it's been two years. The man couldn't seem to get his life together."

We seemed to have broken the ice with the old cowboy and wanted to keep him talking. "Any idea who'd want to kill him?" I asked.

"Nah, I didn't know him that well. He rented the trailer out back." The older man pointed through the trees. I could barely make out a mobile home. "He kept mostly to himself, working all night in this garage. No idea what concoction he was trying to cook up. I kept my distance."

I took a closer look at the drawings. I had no idea what Brent had been up to either, but it looked complex.

"I won't save it for you. If Donovan beats you to it, he can have it. First come, first serve."

"Donovan Cavalier?" Vance clarified.

"Yep, that's him. I always make tenants list next of kin. You never know when they're going to skip town or wind up dead."

"Good thinking. Well, we won't keep you. Thank you for your time." I took one last look at the workshop and then followed Vance to the truck.

"THERE'S a Donovan Cavalier with a Harrisville address," I said as Vance navigated out of the driveway.

"Do you want to stop by and see what he says?"

"I think that's a good idea. Brent didn't glow when he was in Honor's shop, right?"

"No, I didn't see anything," Vance confirmed. Mortals glowed when they were in Silverlake. It's how witches knew not to perform magic in front of them. Sure, our town had plenty of magical shops with corresponding names like Spellbinding Books, but if a mortal tourist wound up in town, they'd think it was all in good fun. Even mortals who believed in magic and tried to practice it had no idea of the true power a witch could summon.

"Okay, so it stands to reason that Donovan knows about magic," I surmised, because if Brent was a supernatural, so was Donovan.

"Unless he's not biologically related to Brent like a step-brother or something."

"True. I guess I shouldn't make assumptions." I plugged Donovan's address into my phone's map software and let it navigate us to Brent's brother's house.

I called the Sheriff's department along the way and filled them in on Brent's workshop. They'd want to get a unit out there right away to catalog the evidence.

Vance whistled when we turned into the plantation community. I knew Harrisville had its wealthy neighborhoods, but I had never been to one of them.

The neighborhood was tucked away in a secluded corner of the city, surrounded by lush greenery and tall oak trees. The houses were grand and imposing with expansive lawns and perfectly manicured gardens. The neighborhood's architecture could be described as a traditional southern style. Homes had large columned facades, elegant porticos, and gleaming white paint. The roofs were primarily gabled or hipped, and the windows were large and adorned with shutters. The houses were surrounded by tall hedges, which gave the neighborhood a sense of privacy.

Vance parked at the curb and met me at the end of the driveway. Taking his hand in mine, he led us up the smooth concrete and around the brick pathway until we stood on the expansive front porch. Before we could knock, a woman answered the door. She wore a crisp blue button-down shirt tucked into a navy utility skirt. She had thick, shiny pantyhose and short white socks tucked into a pair of brilliant white shoes.

"How may I help you?" she asked with a hawkish expression. Based on her attire and her no-nonsense attitude, I got the feeling she was the housekeeper.

"Good afternoon, my name is Vance Blackwell, and this is my fiancé, Angelica. We were wondering if Mr. Cavalier is home."

"I'm sorry, but this is a no-soliciting neighbor-hood." The woman went to shut the door. I put my foot out to stop it.

"Let's try this again, my name is Deputy Nightingale, and I'm here to talk to Mr. Cavalier about his brother's death." I gave a level stare at the woman.

She looked taken aback but quickly recovered. "Oh, well, just a moment then. Let me see if Mr. Cavalier's accepting visitors."

She shut the door and disappeared down the hallway.

"Sorry, I didn't even think to go with that angle," Vance whispered.

"No, why should you?" I never dropped the deputy credentials, but I had to admit there was something intoxicating about the power of a badge, especially when you used it to solve crimes and take down bad guys. I would never be a deputy full-time, but I rather liked being a part-time one.

"Mr. Cavalier will see you now," the woman said, opening the door and stepping back to allow us to enter the polished wood foyer.

We didn't have far to go as Mr. Cavalier's office was right off the entryway behind a set of French doors. Once again, the woman opened the door and ushered us inside. Mr. Cavalier sat behind an over-sized mahogany desk. He wore a thin gray pinstripe suit with a burgundy pocket square. His gray hair was clipped short and the top gelled into place. His steel-colored eyes followed us as we approached his desk. As if he suddenly remembered his manners, he stood up with one hand tucking his tie close to his body, and he reached across the desk to shake Vance's hand and then mine. His handshake was just enough to make me feel uncomfortable. His grip was too firm, and he held on for a second too long. Mr. Cavalier wanted to make it known that we were in his territory. I cocked my head and wondered if perhaps this man were a shifter. If he were, he'd be an alpha.

"Mrs. Evans tells me you're here on police busi-ness?" The man sat back down. We followed suit, taking up the leather chairs in front of his desk.

Vance looked at me to answer. "That's right. I'm a deputy for Silverlake." I dropped the name of our magical town to see how Mr. Cavalier would react.

Magical enchantments protected the town, but if he were a supernatural like I thought he was, then surely, he'd heard of us, especially being one town over.

"I see. What can I do for you?"

"First, I wanted to share my condolences on the loss of your brother." Mr. Cavalier flicked his hand away as if he were shooing away a fly. "Care to explain that?" I asked, motioning to his gesture.

"Brent got what he deserved. If you play with fire, you'll get burned. He never learned."

"And what exactly was he doing?" Vance asked.

"Going after power, of course. Not everyone likes to be a little brother." Mr. Cavalier held my gaze as he answered Vance's question. I licked my suddenly dry lips. I felt like I was very much in the sights of a predator at that moment.

I found my voice. "Can you give us anything more specific?" I didn't like how the man seemed to talk in riddles while staring me down.

"Did you see his workshop?" Mr. Cavalier asked. I nodded. "I'm sure the answer is there. I don't know what spell backfired on him, but it was more than he could handle. Then again, that's not saying much." Mr. Cavalier stood. "Now, if you'll excuse me, I have a business dinner to attend."

I stood, ready to follow Mr. Cavalier out and hopefully get him to answer a couple more questions. "One more thing—"

Mr. Cavalier rounded on me. His glare choked the words in my throat. "You listen here. Brent got what he deserved. He could never handle the hierarchy of the pack; never accepted his place. The only one responsible for his death is him."

I nodded. Vance's hand came up to the small of my back, encouraging me to keep quiet. He didn't have to worry; I had no intention of arguing with the alpha.

"Thanks for your time," I managed to say.

"Have a good night," Vance said over my head.

We saw ourselves out.

Chapter 8

"That was interesting," I said as I clicked my seatbelt in place. I couldn't erase the feeling of unease. I felt like I had just been in the presence of a dangerous predator. The way he looked at me, the way he spoke in riddles, and the way he dismissed his brother's death all made me feel like there was more to this story than he was letting on. I knew we were getting closer to the truth about Brent's death, but I also couldn't shake off the feeling that we were getting closer to something dangerous and deadly.

"Who knew Donovan was an alpha?" Vance said.

"That would explain the wealth." Alphas oversaw a particular territory which often included owning various businesses. To mortals, they looked like successful and powerful businessmen and women. Alphas could be male or female. The honor was passed down from generation to generation until an alpha was challenged and defeated.

"It helps paint a bigger picture of Brent." Vance navigated us out of the ritzy neighborhood and back to the real world

"Let me know what you think, but to me, it sounds like Brent was kicked out of the pack for not submitting to his brother's authority."

Vance nodded. "And Brent spent his time doing whatever he could to gain power."

"But is that how he died? Was he trying to make a charm that contained a lot of power, and somebody else found out and killed him for it?"

"That's not a bad theory."

"But who? Did Donovan kill him because he didn't want to be challenged?"

"I don't know. Donovan didn't seem to think Brent was a threat."

"Or he was lying."

"Good point."

"But if not Donovan, then who else is there?" I asked.

"We should've asked him if he knew any of Brent's friends."

"I think he was done answering questions," I grumbled.

Vance chuckled. "That's true. You know I would protect you to the ends of the earth, but I didn't want to get in a fight with an alpha over an interview."

"Aww, c'mon now, we could've taken him," I joked, acting braver than I had felt in the man's presence. Never mind that Donovan's pack would've retaliated against us. Everyone got along together really well in Silverlake, but I knew that wasn't the way of the outside world. Witches and shifters often avoided one another. Each had its own set of politics and power plays.

"We should look into Brent's background more. Dwayne said Brent was living there since his divorce. Maybe his ex-wife has something to do with his death?"

"That's a good idea. She might also know who he's friends with."

▭

IT WAS GETTING close to dinner time. Vance and I had planned on going to a restaurant for dinner, but those plans changed when Deputy Jones was able to get us the ex-wife's name and address. Brooklyn Horgel owned a nail salon in Harrisville, and if we hurried, we could get there before she closed. Thankfully, Aunt Thelma was more interested in us solving this case than in me working, and she picked up my evening shift.

"How about you wait out in the car while I go in

and scope things out?" I suggested to Vance when he pulled into the parking lot. The nail salon was located in a small corner unit of a bustling strip mall. The storefront was adorned with a large front window with the salon's name etched on the front of it. A separate sign above the door was eye-catching, with bold, colorful letters that spelled out *NAILS*. Twinkling fairy lights were wrapped around the windows and door, adding a touch of festivity to the entrance.

"Sounds good. I'll park off to the side here."

"What can I do for you, sweetie?" A beautiful brunette with full lips and a warm smile glanced up at me when I walked in. The woman was gluing on acrylic nails to the older woman sitting in front of her. "Hi, I'm looking for Brooklyn?"

"That would be me. Are you looking at a fill or a full set?"

I looked down at my nails. They were chipped, cracked, and looked nothing like what a bride's nails should look like. If I were getting married this weekend, it would be nice to have a manicure.

"Manicure if you have time."

"Have a seat. I'll be with you in about fifteen minutes."

I took a seat off to the side in the small waiting area and shot Vance a text telling him my plan.

The salon was small but cozy. The walls were painted a pale pink, and the floors were covered in a neutral-colored tile. The salon had a handful of pedicure chairs with two guests in them, and a few manicure stations with comfortable chairs. Each station had a small Christmas decoration like a snowman or a reindeer on it. I picked up an entertainment magazine off the coffee table to waste the time. It had been ages since I'd tuned into Hollywood gossip. I had no idea who was even famous anymore.

Brooklyn was true to her word and was done with her client in just under fifteen minutes. The woman sat off to the side, drying her nails under one of the shop's UV light boxes. It was the kind you slipped your hand into while a timer off to the side counted down how many minutes you had left.

"I don't think I've seen you around here before," Brooklyn said as she led me to her station and offered me a seat.

"It's a long story." While I waited, I decided to go with the truth versus coming up with some story and trying to fish information out of her. I'd rather tell Brooklyn how I tracked her down before she started painting my nails instead of having her kick me out with one hand half done when I started questioning her about her ex. You never knew how people will react when you bring up their divorce. Brooklyn cocked her head to the side and waited for me to elaborate. "I'm a local deputy and I'm working on your ex-husband's case. I also happen to be getting married this weekend, and my nails could use some help."

"Case? What's Brent gone and done now? He's always coming up with some harebrained scheme or another. Where'd you say you were deputy at again?" The woman kept her voice low.

Again, I went with the truth. "In Silverlake."

"That's what I thought. I got the witch vibe off of you. I'm the same, although potions are my specialty. I'm not as good as that Connie of yours, but I'm getting there. Anyway, like I said, what did Brent do?"

"I'm sorry. I don't know why I assumed you had already heard. It must be from living in a small town, but your ex-husband was found murdered last night in Silverlake."

"Murdered. What? Are you sure?"

"I don't want to be too graphic, but I found him strangled with a strand of Christmas lights at the tree lighting ceremony."

"My heavens. You know, we had a downright nasty divorce, and I wished the man out of my life, but I didn't think the universe would answer with something quite so drastic." Brooklyn seemed to think for a minute before saying, "So, that's why you're here? You want to know what I was doing last night?"

"No, not it at all. I don't think anyone's considered you a suspect." Only the future would tell if that was a mistake or not. "I was stopping by to see if you knew anyone who might have had it out for him? Or maybe who his friends were? I just stopped by and talked to his brother a minute ago."

Brooklyn rolled her eyes and held her hand out for me to put my hand in hers. I took it as a good sign that she was willing to go forward with the manicure.

"Donovan Cavalier. That man oozes power and authority. Some women find it sexy as all get out, but you know what? I don't like being dominated like that. That's what happened with Brent and me. He started trying to act controlling, and I wasn't having that. I'm an independent woman, you know what I'm saying? I built this business from the ground up. I'm self-sufficient. I don't need a man telling me what time to be home, what I can wear, or what I should eat. Brent had another thing coming if he was going to talk to me that way. He wanted to be his brother so bad when in reality, he was a much better man than Donovan was any day."

"Did you tell him that?"

"Oh, I tried, but you know how shifters are. It's all about the pecking order, and some men just want to be on the top. It was a shame, but I knew a lost cause when I saw one. I couldn't force Brent to be the man he used to be just like he couldn't make me submit."

"When was the last time you saw him?"

"I didn't see him much around town. I know he was renting a trailer there off of Dixie. He tended to keep to himself." Brooklyn got back to work on my nails. We were silent for a few minutes. "You know what, though? I did see him with that sweet redhead not that long ago." I leaned in to make sure I heard the woman correctly. "Shoot, what's her name? She's a local girl, a witch too." Brooklyn stopped filing my nails and leaned back to holler over at the receptionist. "Kitty, what's the girl's name who was dating Brent? The pretty redhead."

"Elizabeth." Kitty held her hand over the receiver of the telephone and shouted back. "Elizabeth Webb."

My jaw about hit the floor. I knew Elizabeth Webb. She was the witch working with Cassidy at the apothecary.

"By the look on your face, you know who she is," Brooklyn said.

"I do. I'll check in with her after this."

Chapter 9

Vance and I ended up getting fast food on our way home. I filled him in on everything Brooklyn said along the way.

"He was dating Elizabeth?"

"That's what Brooklyn said. She also showed me her appointment book to prove that she was working last night. She gave me the names and numbers of the clients too. I guess their divorce got pretty bad. She said she might not be a suspect yet, but that was only because I hadn't talked to any of his friends yet." Brooklyn gave me two names of Brent's friends, Andrew Tanner and José Riddle. She wasn't sure if they were close anymore, but they had been when they were married.

"At least she's honest."

"A bit too honest. She said if she had a chance,

she would've poisoned him. Potions are her specialty."

"Note: never eat or drink anything Brooklyn gives you."

"But my nails are lovely." I turned my perfectly polished pink nails in the air so Vance could admire them.

"So, Elizabeth Webb?"

"I figure I can talk with her tomorrow now that she lives in town, or here, while I'm thinking about it, let me text Deputy Jones. He can relay the info, and maybe another deputy will want to try to catch up with her tonight." It was amazing what you could get done when you worked as a team and weren't actively working against the sheriff every step along the way.

Vance and I were both dead on our feet by the time we got back in Silverlake. Vance dropped me off at the inn, and I promised I would check in with him tomorrow before heading out to interview anyone. We planned to meet up tomorrow night with Aunt Thelma and Clemmie to see how the alternative wedding plans were coming. If there was power in positive thinking, I was going to do my best to think happy thoughts that the wedding would still happen this weekend.

"Good night, Percy," I said to the poltergeist who worked behind the front counter. Percy had always worked the night shift. Being a ghost, he didn't need to sleep. He and his wife, Eleanor, were the perfect dream team. Neither one minded working throughout the night, and they were both good at their jobs. No one could clean like Eleanor. After spending two hundred years tidying her small apartment above the tavern, having the entire inn to clean brought her such joy. I had never seen someone so happy to go room to room, straightening everything up and making it just right. Maybe it wasn't cleaning that Eleanor loved as much as she loved being free. She hadn't hung around the tavern for generations because she'd wanted to. She'd been cursed by a crazed witch named Tabitha, who didn't take too kindly to Eleanor jilting her son. However, all of that was long in the past. Eleanor was now free and in love. Percy couldn't have married a better ghost. I had no complaints, either. Eleanor kept Percy in line. I hadn't found a dead fish in my bed for the last three months.

"Hey, Jelly," Percy said, using my nickname from when I was a kid. The poltergeist had come with the inn when my aunt acquired it forty years ago.

"Heard you almost got blown up today. That would've been gruesome, huh? Not to worry, though. If you ever do get blown to smithereens, I'll show you all the cool haunts. Get it? The cool haunts?"

"Oh, come now, Percy. Poor girl had quite a

fright," Eleanor said, materializing beside her husband with a feather duster in her hand.

"It's okay. I'm just glad I wasn't hurt. Any word on how Mr. McCormick and Mrs. White are doing?"

"Mr. McCormick's resting comfortably at home. I ran into his daughter Molly at the market. I don't know how Mrs. White is doing, the poor lady," Eleanor said.

I thought maybe I could send some flowers to the sweet older woman. I didn't have a childhood memory in the library that didn't involve her. She also had helped out on a case or two. Never underestimate the lengths a librarian will go to obtain knowledge. I told Eleanor my idea.

"I'll get right on it in the morning," she said.

"Thank you, I appreciate it. Now you two don't work too hard. I'm off to bed. I'll see you guys in the morning."

"Wait, before you go. I promised Diane I'd save a cookie for you." Percy held up a plate of cookies wrapped in plastic wrap. I knew better than to take anything from Percy.

"They are delicious," Eleanor agreed. Ever since Connie had created a potion that enabled Percy and Eleanor to taste food again, they were sampling desserts left and right. "Take them, please, before we eat them all."

Now, Eleanor, I trusted. I walked the short

distance to the counter and picked up the plate of cookies Percy had hovering in the air. They were snowman cut-out cookies with white frosting and what looked like mini chocolate chips for eyes and mouth. Diane's cookies were the best.

I slipped one of the cookies out and took a bite. The moment I did, Percy hooted with laughter. A large chunk of the cookie stuck to the roof of my mouth like glue; only it wasn't glue, it was toothpaste. Percy had used toothpaste in place of frosting.

I attempted to use my tongue to peel the cookie from the roof of my mouth before beelining to the trash can to throw it away.

"What is wrong with you?" Eleanor asked her husband. She rushed over to my side. "I promise you they tasted perfect when Diane dropped them off!" I spit the cookie into a napkin and threw the other half away. My eyes watered from filling my mouth with that much toothpaste. "You say you're sorry, Percival. Right. This. Minute!"

But the poltergeist wasn't listening. He was too busy flying through the air laughing like an old fool.

I shook my head as Eleanor continued to apologize on behalf of her husband and scold him at the same time. It wasn't her fault. As I said, I knew better, but I didn't want to stay and chat. I wanted to get upstairs and rinse my mouth out, pronto.

I waved my goodbye and hightailed it up the stairs. My plan was to thoroughly rinse out my mouth, take a shower, and head straight to bed. The adventures of the day had caught up to me, and I was ready to get some shut-eye, but that was before I walked in and Aunt Thelma had just finished brewing a pot of tea.

"Care to join me, dear?"

I held up my finger as I walked past her and into the bathroom to rinse out my mouth.

I rejoined her a few minutes later.

"What was that all about?"

"Percy. Don't eat the snowman cookies."

"Noted. As I said, care to join me for tea?"

"I was going to head to bed, but one cup wouldn't hurt." It might even help get rid of the overpowering mint flavor still in my mouth.

"I wasn't planning on making any tea, but then I couldn't find my wand, and by the time I'd searched high and low, I found myself parched. Wouldn't you know it? My wand was right in the teapot."

I shook my head. It wasn't the first time my aunt had found her wand in an unusual location.

"How did your day go?" Aunt Thelma poured the tea, and then I followed her into the living room. My aunt's apartment was styled like the nineteen sixties with pink shag carpet and gold accents. Aunt Thelma was still dating Frederick, the former mayor of Mount Holly. He was coming into town tomorrow for the wedding. I had a feeling he'd be spending more time in Silverlake once I moved out.

As it was now, the couple split their time between the two towns.

I didn't have much to move when I moved out next week into Vance's apartment. I'd sold everything in Chicago when I moved back home. The current plan was for me to move into Vance's, and then we would start house hunting in the spring when his lease was up. There wasn't much currently on the market, but I was hopeful the perfect property would pop up.

I told my aunt about the twists and turns of the day from finding out that Brent was a shifter to meeting his ex-wife and her telling us about Elizabeth.

"It sounds like you had an eventful day. I bet you didn't think about the wedding once." My aunt winked, reminding me that was her plan all along.

"Maybe once or twice." I flash my aunt my manicure. "But you were right. Focusing on Brent's case helped me take my mind off of things." My mood sobered. "Did you hear anything about the explosion?"

My aunt shook her head. "Only town gossip. Mrs. White swears she heard someone cackling in the air, but I think it was probably her ears ringing from the explosion."

"Cackling? I didn't hear anything, but you know how close I was."

"Too close. I'm going to say extra prayers

tonight." My aunt reached over and squeezed my hand before letting go.

"How did it go today? Did you find a new venue for the wedding?" I winced, waiting for the shoe to drop.

"I did."

"You did?"

"Mm-hm, and if you trust me, it'll be the most beautiful wedding you've ever been to." My aunt beamed.

"Really? Where?"

"I think it would be best for it to be a surprise. Clemmie agrees."

I bit my bottom lip as I thought about it. "Is it at the bed-and-breakfast?"

"No, although we did consider it. Shannon's backyard is lovely." The bed-and-breakfast was the home of the town's former mayors. Every mayor in Silverlake lived there while they were in office until Mayor Parrish held the title. She refused to step foot in the "drafty" Victorian, preferring her luxury condo instead. It all turned out for the best as Shannon Prescott turned the home into a lovely B&B.

"What about Wishing Well Park?" Couples occasionally hosted weddings in the park. They would set up an oversized white tent that was big enough for a dance floor and a band and string white lights from the mature pecan trees.

"Nope, not the park."

If it wasn't at the church, bed-and-breakfast, or the park, I wasn't sure where else it could be. "It's not the tavern, is it?" I scrunched my nose.

My aunt chuckled. "No, it's not the tavern."

"Hmmm. I'm stumped then."

"And I know how much you love a good mystery."

"That's true, I do."

"Let's see if you can solve it before Saturday."

"A challenge. I like it."

"I thought you might."

"Okay, well, if you're convinced you found the perfect location, I'll leave it to you and Clemmie to work your magic."

"Are you and Vance still able to meet with us tomorrow? I have a decision or two for you to weigh in on."

"Yes, we're planning on it."

"Okay, dear. If you don't mind, I think I'm going to take my tea and retire to my room. There's a new Jenna St. James novel out that I can't wait to read. I just love that Witch in the Woods series of hers."

"Enjoy. I'm going to turn in too. Thanks for the tea. I'll see you in the morning."

It didn't take long for me to fall asleep even with my mind trying to piece together where Aunt Thelma was planning on hosting the wedding. The Simmering Spoon was a nice upscale restaurant. I could see hosting a reception there, but there wasn't really space for an actual ceremony. Our original plan was to have the ceremony at the church and then come back to the inn for the reception. As far as I knew, that was still the plan.

That was the last thing I remembered until whiskers tickling my chin woke me up. At least, that's what it felt like. I brushed the stray hairs away and thought briefly that I might've transformed into Penelope in my sleep again. That happened from time to time, especially when I was stressed. I twitched my nose and felt my fingertips against my smooth skin. No, I was definitely still me. I rolled over and tugged the comforter with me, burying myself deep into the pillow.

I must have just barely drifted back off to sleep when I felt the whiskers against my skin once more. I brushed them away and started to think maybe there was something scratching me on my comforter. I loosened my grip on the bedding and hoped that that would remedy the problem. It was right then, at that moment, that I felt tiny little teeth bite down on my earlobe.

Instant pain throbbed in my ear. "Ah!" I swatted the furry intruder off my ear and sent it flying across the bedroom. It landed on the floor with a soft plop. It was then that I realized my room was quickly filling with smoke.

Flames licked at the walls and ceiling. The

curtains were ablaze. The sound of the fire was deafening, crackling and popping as it devoured everything in its path. My mind raced, trying to think of a way to put out the fire. The mouse squeaked like a maniac from the floor, and I knew it was telling me to get out. In seconds the room was engulfed in flames. Smoke choked the air out of my lungs and stung my eyes.

I slipped off the bed and kept low to the ground, crawling to where I knew the bedroom door was. It was shocking how quickly the smoke overtook me. It was like I was trapped in a magical inferno, and I was about to become toast.

Whomever my mouse friend was, they kept close to my side, guiding me in front. I could just make out their furry backside as we made it to the door. My heart pounded in my chest, fear and adrenaline pumping through my veins. I had to get out of here before it was too late.

I put the palm of my hand on the corner of the door to make sure it wasn't hot and lifted up on my knees to turn the knob. That was a mistake. The metal was searing hot. "Ah, son of a gun." I quickly ripped off my shirt and used it to wrap around the knob, and opened the door. The rest of the apartment was smoke-free, but it wouldn't be long before the fire ripped through the entire inn. I ran down the hall and banged on Aunt Thelma's door before turning around to look for the mouse, who was long gone. Wasting no time, I opened my aunt's bedroom door and shouted at her to wake up. With how quickly the fire was spreading, it was going to take more than my aunt and I with a couple of wands to put the blaze out. We needed the fire department here immediately, and we needed to evacuate everyone before somebody got hurt. My aunt and I ran out of the apartment. She tossed her robe at me along the way so I could cover my top half. We pulled the first fire alarm we came to and then proceeded to bang on the doors as we ran down the hall, telling everyone there was a fire. Percy and Eleanor joined in, making sure everyone knew to get out. It was utter madness.

Chapter 10

I stood in the parking lot of my family's inn, surrounded by guests in their pajamas and robes, shivering in the cold December weather. The smell of smoke and the sound of sirens filled the air as Fire Chief Grady and his team worked to put out the remaining flames. My heart felt heavy as I tried to assess the damage. This was not just any building; it was my family's home. I prayed it would be okay. I couldn't believe this was happening. I felt like I was in a nightmare, but I knew it was all too real.

After the last of the flames were extinguished, Chief Grady approached me. I had just finished talking to a nice couple in town from Atlanta. They'd come to Silverlake for a little holiday rest and relaxation and to get in a bit of Christmas shopping. Aunt Thelma and I were doing our best to reassure guests everything was under control when, in reality, we had no idea.

"We've found something I need to show you." The fire chief kept his voice low.

"What is it?" I whispered back.

"It's probably best to show you." He led me towards the entrance of the inn, where a group of firefighters was huddled around a phone. The smell of smoke and ash filled my nose. The firefighter held up his cell phone for me to see. Written in soot on the bathroom mirror were the words *I'm back.*

I felt a chill run down my spine. I've put a lot of bad guys away over the past two years, and I couldn't help but wonder who was back for revenge. I scanned the faces of the guests behind me, trying to see if anyone looked suspicious, but everyone looked just as shocked and confused as I felt.

"What did they find?" Aunt Thelma asked as she came to stand next to me.

The fire chief shared the phone screen with her. My aunt gasped.

"It wasn't an accident?"

"No, ma'am, doesn't look that way, but I'm not sure how it was started. We're lacking evidence." The fire chief motioned to Sheriff Reynolds.

"No sign of forced entry. No igniting fuel either," the sheriff explained.

I nodded, unable to speak. The fact that the fire

was able to start without any known cause made it all the more terrifying.

"What else aren't you saying?" Aunt Thelma asked, sensing there was more to the story.

"That fire was like nothing we've ever battled before. With how hot it was, it should've burned down the entire inn, but it didn't. It only destroyed Angelica's bedroom."

"The rest of your inn is as good as new," the sheriff agreed.

"Are you telling me it was a spell?" Aunt Thelma asked.

"No other explanation," the chief replied.

I stood there, feeling a mix of emotions from anger to fear. Someone was after me, and I didn't know who. The only thing I knew was I needed to talk to Vance and the rest of my friends as soon as possible. We needed to figure out who could have done this and take them down once more. I couldn't let my family and guests be put in danger again.

Vance soon arrived with Clemmie right behind him. They both had worried expressions on their faces, and I could tell they were relieved that we were okay.

"What happened?" Vance asked as he hugged me tightly.

"I'm not even sure if I can explain it." I felt dazed.

"We need an emergency meeting," Aunt

Thelma said, but even as she said the words, she looked back at the inn. She couldn't go anywhere. She had plenty of work ahead of her reassuring our guests that everything was okay. I really shouldn't leave either, but Aunt Thelma wouldn't hear otherwise.

"Diane invited us to the bakery," Clemmie said with her phone up to her ear.

I had no idea what time it was, but it had to be early if Diane was already at work.

"Tell her you'll head over right away. I'm going to stay here," Aunt Thelma replied calmly. I opened my mouth to protest once more, but my aunt simply turned and walked away.

I looked down at my clothes, having no idea what to wear, not to mention my wedding dress. It was gone.

That apparently was my undoing.

Vance was immediately by my side, his arms wrapping around me in a comforting embrace once more. "It's okay. We'll get through this. I'm here for you," he whispered, rubbing soothing circles on my back.

I clung to him, feeling like the world was crashing down around me. "My wedding dress, it's gone," I choked out between sobs. "It was in my room, and now it's gone."

Vance pulled back and looked at me, his eyes full of understanding and empathy. "We'll get you another dress. It doesn't matter what you wear as long as I get to marry you," he said, wiping away my tears with his thumb.

I nodded, trying to take comfort in his words. I knew he was right it was just a dress, but it still felt like a small piece of my heart had been ripped out. I looked around at the destruction and felt a wave of sadness wash over me. It was just one more thing that hadn't gone right.

IT TURNED out it was after five o'clock in the morning, which explained why Diane was already at work. She usually got to the bakery around four. It was still pitch black out. The sun wouldn't greet the horizon for a couple more hours. I looked up into the cloud-covered sky. The clouds were so thick they obscured the entire nighttime sky. I couldn't spot a single star to wish upon.

When we walked into the bakery, Misty, Luke, Diane, and her husband, Roger, were waiting for Vance, Clemmie, and me.

Misty wrapped me in a fierce hug. "I'm killing whoever did this," she declared.

"Going to have to get in line," Vance replied.

"I think we'd all like to murder the person behind this," Clemmie added.

"It's not right. They deserve to pay," Luke agreed.

I expected Diane to say something, but she was too busy. Diane was always so cool and calm, but she was fussing around the bakery like a honeybee at the height of summer. I watched her as she gathered a plate of scones followed by a mixed plate of danishes and doughnuts. Then she quickly filled two carafes of coffee before loading up a tray and carrying it to the small tables where we were assembled.

"What are you doing? You don't have to wait on us," Clemmie said as she helped Diane unload her tray. "I'm sorry, I can't help it. I agree with Roger; it's just not right. I swear if I don't keep busy, I'll go crazy, and it's not even me the person's after."

I looked around the room. Everyone seemed so upset and frustrated on my behalf. I could feel the anger rolling off of them at the injustice of the situation. My heart swelled. This was my tribe. These people were ready to go to battle for me. How did I get so lucky to have such an amazing group of friends?

I quickly got down to business before I turned emotional. "You guys agree with me; the whole *I'm back* thing means it's probably someone I put away before."

"That makes the most sense." Luke reached across the table and grabbed a chocolate-filled donut off the stack. Diane didn't even bother asking who wanted coffee. She brought out a tray of mugs and began wordlessly pouring us each a cup.

I took a sip of the piping hot brew and felt myself calm a fraction. I hadn't had much of an appetite, but the cream cheese danish staring at me changed my mind. Both the pastry and a glazed doughnut looked pretty good right about then. I started with the danish, but I wasn't making any promises. I figured I had cheated death twice in two days. Calories no longer mattered.

"Any of your bad guys recently been released from prison?" Luke asked before taking a bite.

"No one *should* have been released, that's for sure." Roger sat back and folded his arms across his chest.

I thought back to everyone I'd help put behind bars. "No one should even be eligible for parole."

"You know, I saw a Witch News Investigation once where an ex-husband was behind bars, and he paid a hitman to murder his wife. It was a tricky case. Gruesome too. He scattered her body all over the country. Maybe it's something like that?" Clemmie suggested.

"Scattered her body?" I mouthed the words. Suddenly I envisioned an assassin hiding out in my closet, waiting for me to go to sleep so they could chop me up into pieces. The blood drained from my face.

"Don't tell her that!" Misty said, taking in my horrified expression. "Can't you see you're freaking her out?"

"I'm just saying we have to explore all the possibilities. Criminals are tricky. That explosion at the church was no accident," Clemmie added.

"I know." I'd already come to the same conclusion.

Vance spoke up. "Here's what I think. We need to do some leg work this morning and make sure everyone Angie's put away is still behind bars."

"That shouldn't be hard to find out," Luke agreed.

"No, it shouldn't. The second part requires a bit more work. We need to check phone records and visitation logs. See if any pattern jumps out in case Clemmie's right. Not about the slicing and dicing. About someone working from the inside," Vance added.

"Now you're thinking." Clemmie nodded her approval.

"Luke, can you help me go through the data?" Vance asked.

"I can do that," I offered, trying not to be annoyed Vance didn't think to ask me.

"I know you can, but your safety's more important. We need to come up with something more than your charm necklace," Vance motioned to the charm I had gotten from Honor's shop.

"Listen to the man. He knows what he's talking about," Misty said, siding with Vance.

I glared at my friend. I wasn't going to argue with Vance. I just wasn't used to everyone fussing over me or fearing for my life.

"You know who could probably help? Connie. I'm sure she has a protection potion or spell bubble she can give you," Diane added.

"Connie's a good one," Roger agreed.

"I'll send her a message right now," Diane said, getting out her cell phone.

"I still can't believe this." Suddenly being a deputy and putting away bad guys wasn't so much fun anymore. My friends all looked at me. Their various sympathetic expressions didn't help.

"Any of your past cases jump out at you?" Misty asked.

I knew she was trying to be helpful, but more than one person in my past had tried to kill me. People tended to do that when you uncovered their secrets.

"It could be any of them," Vance said as he sipped his coffee. "You've put a lot of bad guys away."

"I know," I said, feeling a pit in my stomach, "but who would go this far?"

"Someone with nothing to lose," Clemmie said. And I knew she was right.

Chapter 11

I hung out at Diane's bakery for far too long, sampling every single pastry the woman had to offer. Misty stayed with me for moral support while I conjured a new cell phone. Mine was destroyed in the fire.

After ordering and receiving my phone, I filled Misty in on the latest wedding drama and Aunt Thelma's promise she had everything under control. The truth was, as excited as I was for the wedding, I was getting more worried about it every second that someone was going to kill me before I could say I do, or worse yet, strike me dead at the altar. I didn't like the thought of standing in front of my family and my friends with a target on my back. Misty tried to be reassuring, but I could tell she had her doubts.

Connie had promised she would get working on

a potion right away. She told Diane that protection potions took a bit of finesse and asked if I could stop by after eight o'clock. The time was fast approaching.

Vance hadn't explicitly asked Misty to babysit me, but I had a feeling my friends wouldn't let me out of their sight if they could help it. So much for trying to focus on Brent's murder to help take my mind off things. Actually, despite everything going on, I still wanted to find out what happened to Brent and Honor. I just had to be careful about it.

"You're right on time," Connie said when we walked through the door. Connie was at her cauldron behind the counter, stirring a bubbling potion with a long wooden spoon. We approached the counter and peered over the edge. The brew was deep purple, and pink steam rose from the surface. The potion gave off a sweet yet earthy aroma, and I couldn't help but feel a sense of comfort just smelling it.

"Thanks for doing this," I said while watching Connie work. She moved fast. A pinch of this. A dollop of that. The potion bubbled and hissed after each ingredient was added. Connie didn't reply for a moment. She was focused on her work, and I didn't want to interrupt her. I trailed after Misty, taking in Connie's Christmas potion kits. She'd bundled together a mini cauldron with her best-selling potions book and a sample pack of ingredients. The bundles were themed. Green was for luck, red was love, and gold was for prosperity. It was a smart idea. I'd bought a cauldron from Connie a little over a year ago, but it sat unused in Aunt Thelma's kitchen. I should've started with something smaller like this.

"It's done!" Connie called. I left the mini cauldrons and returned to the counter.

"I think you'll like it. It's a protection potion, as promised. I infused it with amethyst for protection, lavender for calming, and a touch of peppermint for a refreshing boost." Connie gave it a final stir.

"How does it work?" Misty asked, rejoining us.

"Think of it like armor. The potion creates a protective barrier around you. It's mostly effective against magical attacks. I don't know if it would stop a bullet. I've never tried, but if someone fires a curse at you, it'll bounce right off." I raised my eyebrows. I really hated it when people shot at me. "You want to try it?"

"Right now?"

"Yep, I just want to do one more thing." Connie took out her wand and said an incantation while waving around the cauldron. The brew bubbled and hissed, reaching a crescendo and sending purple fog wafting into the air.

Two minutes later, Connie handed me a steaming mug while she filled a gallon-size jug with the rest. I'd never noticed the spigot on the back side of her cauldron, custom-made, no doubt. It enabled Connie to easily fill individual bottles.

I took the cup and took a sip of the potion. It was warm and had a slightly sweet and herbaceous taste like a strong tea. As I drank it, I could feel a sense of peace and security wash over me.

"Back in college I named it my Superman potion because it made me feel invincible." Connie smiled. "Feel better?"

"I do." I exhaled, feeling lighter than I had in days.

"Speaking of superheroes, I have another potion that couldn't hurt. Hang on, give me a minute. This one is from my private stock in the back. I keep it under lock and key."

Misty and I raised our eyebrows at one another. Who knew what potion Connie would come back with?

It didn't take long for her to come back with a slim vial with a twist off top. It reminded me of a perfume sample with how small the container was.

"If you tell anyone you got this from me, I'll deny it. It's illegal. Just in Silverlake," Connie quickly clarified.

"What is it?" I took the shimmering green potion from Connie.

Connie looked around the store to ensure no one had come in while she was in the back before answering, "It's an invisibility potion."

"Invisibility?" Misty and I said with surprise at the same time.

"Ssshh, keep your voice down. Don't make me regret giving it to you."

"Okay, don't worry, we won't say anything."

"It's one of a kind and I don't have any left. I made it after a particularly bad breakup. The guy wouldn't take no for an answer. It freaked me out." Connie let her words hang in the air. I didn't know much about Connie's personal life because she tended to keep to herself, but the situation must have been bad if she had been afraid.

"Anyway, whenever you feel threatened, take a sip – just a sip – and you'll become invisible."

"For how long?" Misty asked before I could.

"Enough time to get away. As soon as your adrenaline wears off, you'll reappear."

"I should've had this years ago," I said to myself more than anyone.

"Unfortunately, Sheriff Reynolds will arrest me if he finds out I made that." Certain potions and spells were against the law. Invisibility potions were one of them. If people could run around invisible all the time, it would be hard to keep law and order. Not only that, but invisibility potions were notoriously tricky. One wrong move and you could disappear forever. It was a good thing I trusted Connie.

It was also a good thing she was a good witch

because I was convinced she was the most powerful person in all of Silverlake.

"How much do I owe you?" I reached for my wallet.

"No charge."

"No, I insist."

"Trust me. It's the least I can do. I'm just glad I can help you in some way. Speaking of which, do you want some help putting extra wards around the inn?

"You know, that's a really good idea."

Misty and I went to leave the shop, and then I thought of something else. I took out my cell phone and scrolled to the photos I took of Brent's workshop. I zoomed in and showed Connie the photos. "Do these symbols mean anything to you?"

Connie scrunched her face while she studied the diagrams. "That would be some black magic there." She pointed at the painted diagram on the floor. "Where is this at?" She took my phone and turned the angle.

"You know the man who was found strangled behind the Christmas tree? His name was Brent Cavalier. This was his workshop outside Harrisville."

"I didn't know you were investigating that case," Misty chimed in.

"I wasn't going to, but then I started to, and now I'm just not sure." My head was all over the place. If

I was still investigating the case, I needed to talk with Elizabeth if Deputy Jones hadn't yet.

"It's starting to make sense now," Connie said while handing my phone back.

"What's making sense?" I asked.

"That guy, Brent? He was in here last week. I remember him because he bought everything for a necromancy potion, and you don't see that every day."

"Eww," Misty remarked from beside me. I had to agree. Necromancy made my skin crawl. It was definitely black magic. You shouldn't mess with the dead.

"Do you know if there's anyone else who might be into that sort of thing?"

"In Silverlake? Are you kidding?" Misty interrupted.

She was right. The people of Silverlake were generally good people. If anyone did practice black magic, they wouldn't be open about it.

"What about in Harrisville?" I amended. "I talked to Brent's ex-wife, but she never brought that up."

"No, not my crowd, but you might want to ask Pauline. That's where she's from."

"Pauline Ruble?" I clarified.

"Yep, that's her. She was born and raised in Harrisville. If anyone knows the area around there, it would be her."

Pauline's name shouldn't have surprised me. I knew the witch was hiding something. It was time to repay her a visit.

"What's the game plan, boss?" Misty asked me as we stepped out of the potion shop.

I scanned the area. Bright sunlight reflected off the pristine white snow. Kids ran around, playing in the conjured pile from Monday night, or maybe it was a fresh batch seeing as it wasn't slushy. The children were bundled up in warm coats and hats, their cheeks rosy from the cold as they threw snowballs and built snowmen. Their laughter filled the air, and I felt a sense of normalcy return to my life for a moment even though I was still holding a gallon of protection potion.

I turned back to my friend and got back to business. "Well, we know Pauline's hiding something."

"We do? What have you not been telling me?"

"Sorry, let me get you caught up to speed." I took a few minutes to give Misty a rundown of how nervous Pauline had been when I stopped in yesterday morning and how the rest of the interviews went.

"Pauline kicked you out," Misty summarized.

"More or less. Between her and Elizabeth, I think we'll be able to crack this case wide open."

"Let's just keep *your* head from getting cracked open in the process."

"Gee, thanks."

"You know I love you. I'm only making light of things so I don't go all ragey."

"I know that."

"How about, when we're done with this, do you want to go dress shopping? Vance told me about your wedding dress."

I sighed. "I'm not sure if I'm up for it or not. You know how much I loved that dress." That dress had been handmade with magic-infused thread said to bless our marriage with a lifetime of love and happiness. It sounded ridiculous and romantic all at the same time. I wanted to believe in happily ever after. It wasn't like I could conjure a replacement. I swallowed the lump that formed in my throat.

"Okay, forget the dress. Let's go take down some bad guys. Do you want to be good cop or bad cop?" Misty smiled broadly at me.

I was about to tell Misty she could take the lead when I saw my little mouse friend sitting along the sidewalk. Technically, it was sitting along the landscaping border next to the sidewalk, but it was the same mouse. I was sure of it. It had bright, beady eyes and a long, skinny tail. Before I could explain, I pushed the gallon of potion into Misty's arms and ran off.

I gave chase.

The mouse scurried across the cobblestone path, pausing to look at me before darting into a nearby alleyway.

I was right behind him.

I had to catch the mouse. They held the answers to who was behind the fire. I ran after it, my heart pounding in my chest.

"Look out!" I shouted to Beatrice and Sabrina. Leave it to the twins to animate a snowman in the center of Village Square. Its dark eyes sparkled in the morning light. Its carrot nose was slightly crooked, and a top hat sat perched on its head. The snowman's body was made of compacted snow with twigs for arms and buttons for eyes. It was a classic, friendly-looking snowman, but as I neared it, I could see it had a mischievous glint in its coal eyes. It was hard to tell if he was friendly or not as I kept my eye on the mouse darting every way, trying to lose me.

The snowman's stick arms were waving frantically above its head as if warning others to stay away. Protection charm or not, the snowman saw me as a threat. He stuck his stick arm out to the side as I ran past and tripped me. I went flying, landing on my belly and crashing into a plastic Santa as if he were home plate.

The mouse was long gone. My jacket was soaked, and my ego was bruised. It took me a minute to realize that I wasn't only wet from the snow. The invisibility potion had broken in my pocket. I sighed in frustration.

"Are you okay?" Sabrina ran over and asked while Beatrice scolded her evil snowman creation.

"Yeah, I'm fine." I sucked in air, willing my lungs to remember how to breathe, and thought animating objects was another thing that should be illegal. Sheriff Reynolds could add it to the list along with invisibility potions, conjuring cash, and erasing people's memories. Come to think of it, Silverlake had a lot of laws. Some spells were illegal for everyone, and others just for regular folks. Town Council members had more leeway. For example, they could disappear and reappear around town. It's how they protected the magical borders.

"What are you doing?" Misty said as she caught up to me.

I turned away from the twins. "It was that crazy mouse again. I swear it's stalking me." The mouse had been at the wand shop and rescued me at the inn, and I wanted to know why. "It's time to get some answers."

We hightailed it to the wand shop. I smiled politely at passersby and tried to keep myself from jogging. I knew Pauline had the answers. She needed to talk.

"Angelica? Misty? What can I do for you?" Pauline chuckled nervously as her attention darted around the store.

I knew my eyes were wild, but I couldn't help it. There was a time to be polite, and there was a time to demand answers. I was done being polite.

"Do you need a new wand?" Pauline asked sheepishly.

"No, I need to talk to you about a mouse. You know, the one you tried to convince me didn't exist? Well, guess what? I know I saw him here yesterday, and I know you lied about it."

Pauline snapped her mouth shut.

"Your mouse friend also saved my life this morning. So, fess up. What's the story?"

Pauline began to sweat on the spot. "I don't know what you're talking about." She couldn't even look me in the eye.

"Oh, come on. You obviously know," Misty spoke up.

Pauline shook her head, refusing to answer.

"Why won't you tell us? What are you so afraid of?" I asked.

"If you need protection, Connie can help you," Misty added.

Pauline looked out the window. "I just… I can't. You guys don't understand."

Finally, I felt like we were getting somewhere. "I don't know; we might. Why not try us?"

"If anyone can understand, it's Angelica," Misty added.

Just when I thought we'd turned a corner, Pauline snapped at us, "Why are you doing this to me? This is harassment! Why won't you leave me alone!" Pauline's voice cracked.

I jumped back. Pauline was right, I had come at her pretty hard, but I wanted answers. Before I could say I was sorry, Pauline winked right out of existence.

POOF!

Misty turned and looked around the store. "What in the world? She can't do that."

"You mean she shouldn't do that." Only Town Council members were allowed to pop in and out of places. Not only was it the law, but it was also dangerous magic. You had to know what you were doing to disappear from one place and pop up in another. I hadn't realized the witch was packing that much power.

"Well, you were right about one thing," Misty said with her hands on her hips.

"What's that?"

"Pauline is absolutely hiding something."

"I know." I sighed.

"It's got to be big, too. She just totally abandoned her job."

"What's so bad that she's willing to break the law and lose her job to get out of it?"

"Whatever it is, it's not good. Let me call Peter and see what he wants us to do." I waited for Misty to call the shop's owner and fill him in. He asked if Misty could stay until another employee could come in. Misty agreed. Even though their relationship hadn't worked out, it was nice to see they'd remained friends.

"While you're here, I'm going to pop over to Cassidy's shop and see if Elizabeth is there." Fingers crossed she'd be willing to talk.

Chapter 12

It turned out that Elizabeth wasn't at the apothecary. Cassidy said she would tell her to call me. I thanked her and went over to Vance's. I was going to have to quit calling it his place soon. I shook my head. I couldn't wait to find a home we both loved.

Vance was still at the office with Luke. I was right; everyone I'd put away in jail was still there. On the one hand, that was a relief, but on the other, that meant it would be harder to track down who was after me. Vance said he'd bring his work home and meet me there shortly. I decided I'd take a quick nap on the couch when I got there. I was tired and never thought clearly when I was sleep-deprived. I called Deputy Jones on my way to Vance's and told him about Pauline's disappearing act and the suspicious mouse. He was going to head to her house to question her. I figured he had a better chance of getting her to talk. I'd tried twice and struck out. He also stopped by Elizabeth's last night, but she hadn't been home. He'd try her place again.

"Oh, and Connie mentioned Brent was into necromancy."

"Necromancy? Now there's something that should be illegal."

"I feel the same way. Not sure if it helps with the case, but I wanted to pass it on."

With Deputy Jones on the case, I could sink into the soft, worn leather of Vance's couch and doze off.

Two hours later, I woke to Vance's phone ringing. He was sitting at the dining room table and moved to silence it immediately.

"Sorry," he whispered when I woke up.

"No, it's okay. I needed to wake up."

I looked at my phone to see what time it was. I stood and walked over to Vance. Aunt Thelma had thrown us a wedding shower a few weeks back, and all of the presents were currently stacked around the dining room. Vance's apartment didn't have room for all of it. Our friends had been generous.

"Are you hungry? I have a couple of Italian subs in the fridge."

"Yeah, I can eat." The sugar rush from my morning pastry feast was long gone. Vance stood, walked over to the fridge, and retrieved two sandwiches wrapped in parchment paper. I followed him and grabbed napkins and sodas. Vance brought the sandwiches and a bag of chips to the kitchen counter.

"How'd your morning go?" he asked.

I told him about Connie's protection potion, chasing the rogue mouse, Pauline disappearing, and still not catching up with Elizabeth in between bites of my sandwich. Italian subs were my favorite. I loved the combination of salami, provolone cheese, lettuce, and tomato topped with oregano and vinaigrette. "Oh, and apparently, Brent was into necromancy, which gives me the heebie-jeebies." Ghosts didn't bother me; after all, Percy lived with me my entire life, but summoning the dead for black magic was a big no in my book. It wasn't against the law to summon dead people. It's what you did with them once they were here that was often illegal. Most necromancers weren't summoning little old ladies for afternoon tea parties.

"Okay, let's think about this. We knew Brent wasn't a good guy. The first time we saw him, he threatened Honor," Vance started.

I took over. "Then, later that night, he was murdered, and Honor's missing."

"If Honor didn't kill him, she's running from the person who did. That still holds."

"Or she's been kidnapped." My eyes got wide as

an idea took hold. "What if Brent had a partner who killed him and kidnapped Honor?"

"And you think Pauline knows?"

"Right, that would make sense. Maybe the killer is using Honor as ransom, and that's why Pauline can't say anything. If she says something, they'll kill Honor. It makes so much sense!" And explains why Pauline's not talking. My heart was pounding. I felt like we were really onto something.

"But who would be Brent's partner? I don't think it's the ex-wife, and honestly, I don't think it's Elizabeth either." I didn't really think Elizabeth was avoiding us per se; we just hadn't had a chance to catch up. I did have those two other names Brooklyn had given me.

"Okay, so not the ex-wife or ex-girlfriend. What about his brother?"

"He could've been lying."

"Exactly, he might've been telling the truth about Brent being weaker than him, but that doesn't mean he wasn't threatened by him."

I pieced it all together. "Donovan followed Brent to Silverlake, killed him, and then kidnapped Honor to do whatever it was that she refused to do for Brent."

Vance and I looked at one another for a minute. It was the perfect solution.

"Are you thinking what I'm thinking?" I asked Vance.

"We need evidence."

"Exactly. It's time for a stakeout."

———

DONOVAN CAVALIER'S neighborhood wasn't the type of neighborhood you could sit around in a parked car all day without somebody calling the cops. Going under the cover of the night would make things a bit easier, but it wasn't foolproof. I could almost bet every house had a security system. If not a full set of cameras, then a video doorbell, at a minimum. It would've been easier if it were the weekend. With a neighborhood like this and so close to Christmas, you could bet there'd be a Christmas party every weekend, but we weren't that lucky. It was a Wednesday night, and we didn't have time to waste.

We arranged with Clemmie to take her Cadillac as it was a new model and would fit in more with the neighborhood. We were supposed to meet my aunt and Clemmie to talk about wedding details, but after we told them our working theory, they shooed us away and assured us that they had everything under control. Aunt Thelma even had the lead on a dress. She would share the details with me in the morning after she talked some more to the seamstress. That was good enough for me. Working on this case really took my mind off the wedding stress and someone trying to kill me. I'm not sure what that said about my mental state, but again, it was better to deal with other people's problems than my own. Vance hadn't found anything suspicious in the inmates' call logs, and Sheriff Reynolds promised he would continue working that angle.

Vance parked the car a few houses down from Mr. Cavalier's large two-story mansion. The neighborhood was quiet and still with only the occasional car passing by. The only sign of life was warm light emanating from front porches and the occasional window.

"Before I forget, there's something I wanted to talk to you about." Vance had been scanning the neighborhood but stopped and turned his attention toward me. "I know you've always thought of the apartment as my place, and you weren't planning on moving much stuff in, but I want the space to feel like ours even if it's only temporary."

"Okay." I wasn't sure where Vance was going with this, but he was right. I did think of the apartment as his.

"I thought we could take my bedroom furniture and set it up in the guest bedroom and order new furniture for our room."

"I think that's a great idea."

"We don't have to stop with the bedroom. We can get new living room furniture, too."

"Stop right there. I love your couch."

"Okay, the couch stays, but you got to admit I need a new rug, and the coffee table's pretty sad."

I thought of the marked-up oak table. It had seen better days. I smiled. "Okay, you're right. Let's make your apartment our first home."

"Good." Vance reached over, took my hand in his, and brought it to his lips. "I can't wait to marry you."

"I feel the same way."

Vance and I sat in silence for a while, scanning the area for any signs of activity. A pair of squirrels chased each other through the yard next door until they disappeared up a tree into the darkness.

As we continued to watch Donovan's house, the minutes slowly ticked by slowly. I tried not to fidget in my seat, but I'd forgotten how boring stakeouts could be. Vance checked his phone for the hundredth time.

"Do you think he's home?" Vance sat forward in his seat as if he could see better if he did.

"I have no idea. I think it's time to get closer."

Vance nodded. On the way over, we decided to sit back and assess the situation before I transformed into Penelope and scoped the place out. Spying on the shifter was risky. Being a predator, he'd know someone had been on his property. He'd be able to smell me. I could only hope that Penelope smelt different than Angelica. I really had no idea how that worked. I should've asked someone. I know my sense of smell was heightened when I shifted, but I never noticed if I smelled any different.

Vance pulled away from the curb and drove around the corner to the next street. My plan was to turn into a cat, run through the yards, see if anything looked suspicious, and then meet Vance back at the neighborhood's entrance. Vance turned the corner, and I drank a swish of Connie's potion. I'd taken to carrying a little bit with me at all times. I could never be too safe.

"Fifteen minutes," I said to Vance before holding my tiger's eye and saying the transformation spell. The second it was complete, Vance carefully picked me up off the passenger seat, opened his car door, and set me on the ground. I shook myself out from head to tail. It always felt weird being carried around.

I bounded off toward Mr. Cavalier's backyard, and Vance drove away.

As I crept up to Mr. Cavalier's house, my senses were heightened in my feline form. The darkness of the night was no match for my sharp eyes, and I could see the intricate details of the houses in the wealthy neighborhood. Christmas decorations adorned the homes, but they were tasteful and elegant. No cheap plastic decorations or inflatables cluttered the yards. Instead, each house was adorned with traditional wreaths and garlands, twinkling lights, and large red bows.

The frozen leaves on the ground crunched under my paws as I made my way closer to Mr. Cavalier's house. The sound of the wind whistling through the trees and the quiet rustling of squirrels bedding down for the night filled my ears. I crept up to the first-floor windows, peering into the immaculate kitchen. The counters were made of gleaming marble, and high-end appliances shone in the moonlight. I moved on to Ken's office, but it was just as immaculate and orderly. Not a single paper or sticky note cluttered the desk. It was hard to even call it an office. Before I came home, the office at Mystic Inn had stacks of mail, books, and folders covering the desk and overflowing onto the floor, and it still sometimes looked that way if I wasn't careful.

I couldn't see a way to look into the second-story windows, but there weren't any lights on up there. Would Donovan keep Honor prisoner in a regular bedroom? Something told me no. I wasn't even sure he'd keep her in his house; one of his businesses was more like it now that I thought about it. I'd suggest the idea to Vance.

A soft light from a basement window caught my attention. Perhaps I stood corrected. Mr. Cavalier could have Honor in his basement. I crept forward, putting one paw in front of the other, my body hugging the side of the house.

My nose twitched, and I could smell Mr. Cavalier's cologne mixed with another scent. I tried not to sneeze as the cheap perfume overtook my senses. Suddenly having two hundred million odor sensors in my nose wasn't a good thing. I'd take my regular human sense of smell back in a heartbeat.

I shouldn't have looked. The perfume should've been enough of a warning, but the moment my eyes focused through the window, I wish they hadn't. Mr. Cavalier was entertaining a woman who definitely wasn't Honor. She was also definitely naked.

I tried not to meow or howl as I jumped back from the window, my paws trying to cover my eyes as I staggered back on two pawed feet, crashing right into a bush. The bare branches poked through my fur and caused me to jump up like any cat would when faced with an unexpected sensation. I leaped up, all four paws coming off the ground. As soon as I landed, I rocketed out of there. I was a blur of fur, running away from a scene I'd just as soon forget.

"Memory charm. Must use a memory charm," I meowed as I ran back through the neighborhood. As far as I knew, it was only illegal to erase other witches' memories. You were free to alter yours as much as you'd like, and right then, I wanted to alter mine badly.

Chapter 13

Aunt Thelma called while I was trying to come up with the right words to tell Vance what I'd witnessed. My face flamed with embarrassment. Vance tried not to laugh, but he failed miserably. I joined in because it really was a ridiculous situation. "Hello?" I said, the laughter still in my voice.

"It sounds like your stakeout went well?" Aunt Thelma replied.

"Not exactly, but that's okay. What's going on?"

"We're going to have a slumber party tonight," Aunt Thelma said with a cheerful voice.

"We are?"

"Not at the apartment. Despite what Chief Grady said, it still smells dreadful up there even with scent charms. We're staying at Clemmie's. All of us. Strength in numbers, as they say."

I wasn't sure what to say or who all of us were. I figured we'd soon find out.

When we got to Clemmie's, cars were parked all in front of her house. However, her driveway was empty. We pulled on up and parked her Cadillac. From the sidewalk, it looked like Clemmie was hosting a holiday get-together. That's probably what anyone who drove by thought even though it was a weekday. If they peeked in her windows, they wouldn't come away scandalized. I shook my head once more at my bad luck.

As I walked into Clemmie's house, everyone was gathered in the living room. Roger, Diane, Luke, and Daniel were lined up against the wall, watching the action unfold. They were all dressed in comfortable clothing, ready for a workout.

Someone had cast a spell to minimize the furniture, making the room feel much larger. Everything was doll-sized except for the couch cushions. They'd been placed on the ground, serving as a safety net for anyone who might get hit by a spell.

The sound of spells being cast and counterspells filled the room, and I could feel the energy of magic in the air.

"Again!" my aunt said, ignoring our entrance, as she flicked her wrist toward her partner, Misty. My aunt had a grim look on her face, which was unusual for her. She was usually the life of the party, but now she seemed focused and serious. I could tell that she was worried about me and the recent attacks. She had always been a protector, and this was no different.

I watched my best friend duel my aunt. Misty's wand moved fluidly as she shouted out counter-spells. Clemmie acted like a teacher, offering tips and encouragement. I could see that they were all taking this very seriously; their faces were focused and determined.

As I stood there, watching them practice, I couldn't help but feel a sense of pride and admiration. These were my family and friends, and they were willing to put themselves in harm's way to protect me. They were all taking the necessary steps to ensure our safety, and I knew I was in good hands. It was clear they were all dedicated to keeping us safe, and I couldn't help but feel grateful for their support.

"Are you ready to try?" My aunt turned to me when Misty was done. My best friend was sweating and breathing heavily.

"Holy guacamole, your aunt is good," Misty said, catching her breath. Daniel met her and gave her a glass of water.

"Luke and Angelica, let's see what you've got." Aunt Thelma motioned me forward.

"Me?" I wasn't sure about that. I felt like I had a ton to learn, and I didn't like being the center of attention even if everyone was my friend.

"Luke is a master. If you can take him down, you'll be able to take anyone down," Aunt Thelma added.

Oh, great. That was the wrong thing to say. My anxiety spiked and I was about to fake a stomachache when Luke spoke up.

"Actually, do you mind if we work outside? It's getting pretty hot in here." Luke was right; it was toasty in Clemmie's front living room.

"I think that's a good idea," I chimed in.

"Very well. Out back you go," Aunt Thelma instructed.

I followed Luke out back to Clemmie's small fenced-in backyard.

"I don't know about you, but I hate trying to learn something when everyone's watching me," Luke confessed.

"Thanks for that."

"No problem. Do you want defense or offense?" Luke asked.

I thought for a moment, trying to decide which would be more beneficial for me to practice. "Defense," I finally said. "I think it's more important for me to know how to protect myself."

Luke nodded in agreement. "Alright, let's start with some basic blocking spells," he said, raising his wand. "Cementi!" he shouted, and a blast of light shot towards me.

I quickly raised my wand, but my mind went

blank. I couldn't think of a single counterspell. I braced, waiting for the spell to hit, but instead, the spell hit my shield and bounced back toward Luke, who expertly deflected it with a wave of his wand. I'd forgotten all about Connie's protection potion.

"How did you do that?" Luke shook his head.

"It's a potion. Connie made it. I'd forgotten all about it."

"I'd say it's a good one."

"Yeah, nice to know it works, but I still want to practice."

"Absolutely. Are you ready to try again?"

I nodded. "Show me what you've got."

I felt my confidence growing as I continued to practice my defense spells with Luke. He was a patient teacher, and I was grateful for his guidance. Time flew by as we worked on different charms and spells, each one becoming more and more difficult.

"Ready to try a bubble charm?" Luke asked.

"Sure?" I wasn't sure what a bubble charm was.

"I know you have your potion, but in case it fails, or you forget to take it, you want to be able to protect your surroundings. Here, let me show you. The first thing you need to do is to focus your energy on the wand," Luke explained as he held out his wand. "Now, wave your wand in a circular motion and recite the incantation 'Bubbleus protectus'," Luke said as he demonstrated the motion with his wand. "Visualize a protective bubble forming out of the tip of the wand and pushing out."

I picked up my wand and mimicked Luke's motions, reciting the incantation. At first, nothing seemed to happen, but then I felt a tingling sensation in my wand, and a shimmering force field appeared in front of me.

"Great job!" Luke exclaimed. "Now, try to make the bubble bigger and stronger."

I concentrated on my wand and the incantation, and soon enough, the bubble expanded. Except, the moment my concentration slipped, it popped.

"That's an excellent start. Let's try again. Ready?"

By the time we finished, my wand arm was feeling sore, but I was energized and ready to take on whatever came my way.

As we all took a break, Clemmie stepped out with a tray of hot cocoa and cookies. "I thought you all might be getting a bit chilly," she said with a smile. We gratefully accepted the warm drinks and treats, taking a moment to catch our breath and relax.

When we stepped back inside, everyone was just wrapping up. "Great work, everyone," Aunt Thelma said, looking around the room. "I can see that we're all making progress. Let's keep this up, and we'll be ready for anything."

As the night went on, Aunt Thelma was proved

right, and we did end up having a sleepover. We all piled into the living room, getting comfortable on the air mattresses and sleeping bags. Clemmie brought out a big bowl of popcorn, and we put on a movie.

We laughed and talked late into the night, discussing everything from the recent attacks to the upcoming wedding. Clemmie and Aunt Thelma were bursting with excitement. They promised we'd love what they'd planned. After that, we talked about Brent's murder and Honor's disappearance. Clemmie agreed that if Donovan kidnapped Honor, he'd probably keep her somewhere else other than his house. I also brought up Brent's friends, Andrew and José. We should've stopped by their houses tonight instead of coming right to Clemmie's.

"You can't spend every hour of the day investigating," Misty said, reaching over and taking a handful of popcorn.

"True, but what if they have Honor?" I countered.

"Did you check with her sister?" Luke asked.

"Whose sister?" I replied.

"Honor's sister," Luke replied.

"I thought she didn't have anyone in town?" I looked at Clemmie.

"What are you looking at me like that for?"

"You said she's from Texas."

"I know what I said. I never said she didn't have any family in town."

"It was implied."

"By who?" Clemmie asked.

I stopped arguing. I wasn't going to get anywhere.

"Be that as it may, I didn't know she had any family in town." Clemmie shrugged.

I groaned.

"Where's her sister?" Vance asked.

"In Harrisville. Nicole Carls. She owns the new age store."

"The what now?" my aunt asked.

"It's a metaphysical store. You know, for mortals who believe in magic."

"Oh, a woo store!" my aunt exclaimed.

"Stop. I love those stores," Misty chimed in.

"I do, too," I confessed.

"How about we go tomorrow?" Misty offered. "Double date?"

"I have to work in the morning," Vance replied.

"I'm supposed to be in Atlanta. Finally got studio time," Daniel added. Even rockstars had to work when they didn't want to.

"It's okay. We'll go together. I have plenty of protection potion for both of us."

Misty clapped her hands. "Excellent."

As the night wore on, I felt safe and protected,

surrounded by my loved ones and the powerful magic that filled the room. I was grateful for the opportunity to let my guard down even just for a little while. Drifting off to sleep, I couldn't help but feel hopeful for the future. With the support of my family and friends, I knew I could face anything that came my way.

───

I WOKE up to the smell of bacon wafting through the air. I stretched and looked around, taking in the sight of all the air mattresses and sleeping bags strewn about Clemmie's living room. I felt like a teenager again, spending the night at a friend's house. Misty and Daniel were still asleep. I wasn't sure where everyone else was.

I got out of my sleeping bag and made my way to the kitchen, where I found Roger cooking breakfast. He was whistling to himself as he flipped the bacon in the pan. He caught my eye and grinned. "Morning, Angelica. Breakfast will be ready soon," he replied softly.

Just as my stomach rumbled in anticipation, Diane walked in the back door with a tray of baked goods. "I hope you all like croissants and cinnamon rolls."

"Have you already been working?" I asked, rubbing my eyes.

"Bright and early as always," she said, setting the tray down on the kitchen counter.

"They smell wonderful." Just then I eyed the coffeepot. The carafe was full and waiting to be poured. "Coffee?" I asked Diane and Roger.

"Better not, I've already had two cups," Diane replied, getting out plates.

"I'll have one," Roger replied.

I nodded that I heard him and got down two mugs.

Clemmie came out of her bedroom wearing an ivy silk robe and bunny slippers, looking for her morning coffee. "Good morning, everyone," she said, rubbing her eyes. "I had the best sleep last night. Here I thought I wouldn't like having a household full. Shows what I know. Bacon and coffee? You're all more than welcome to stay."

"Morning, Clemmie. Coffee coming right up." I got down a third mug.

After pouring the coffee, I turned to take a seat at the kitchen table. As I took a sip of my coffee, I spotted Vance outside through the window, talking to Deputy Jones. Unease grew in my stomach.

"What's that about?" I said to myself more than anyone.

"Hmm?" Diane asked.

"Deputy Jones is here." I didn't wait for any more questions. I headed toward the door. I didn't want to wake Misty and Daniel, so I went out the back door, the same one Diane had walked through minutes before.

"What's going on?" I asked the deputy. It was colder outside than I'd dressed for. I crossed my arms over my chest. Vance wrapped his arm around my shoulder and pulled me close to his body to keep me warm.

Deputy Jones nodded. "I'll cut right to it. We've found another body."

Deputy Jones' words hit me like a ton of bricks. Another murder. My mind immediately went to Brent and the list of suspects I had compiled. "Who was it?" I asked, trying to keep my voice steady.

"Andrew Tanner, Brent's friend. Not sure how many details you want, but it wasn't pretty," Deputy Jones replied solemnly.

I felt a knot form in my stomach as I processed this new information. Andrew had been on my list of suspects that I wanted to interview. I couldn't believe he had turned out to be a victim. "Where was the body found?" I asked, still trying to piece together the details.

"At Brent's, in his workshop. A symbol was carved into his chest. Still not sure what he was doing there," Deputy Jones replied.

I felt a wave of horror wash over me. The killer was getting more ruthless.

"And Dwayne?" I hoped the old cowboy was okay.

"We worked a memory charm on him. It was the least we could do for the guy."

I nodded, feeling my resolve lock into place. "We need to find this person before they strike again."

"There's more," Deputy Jones looked down.

"More?"

"I found a note taped to the front door when I got here."

"Wait a second. Are these cases all tied together? Could the same person who killed Brent and Andrew be the one trying to kill me?"

"That's what we were out here talking about," Vance replied.

"But how? None of this makes any sense. I'd never met Brent or Andrew, and I'm not involved in dark magic." I exchanged worried glances with Vance. "What did the note say?" My voice was barely above a whisper.

Vance hesitated for a moment before answering, "It said, 'You won't always be together'." Vance's voice was heavy with concern. "It's clear that the killer knows we're trying to protect you."

A cold wave of fear washed over me. The killer was here last night while we were all sleeping peacefully inside. "We need to be more vigilant than ever." My voice sounded calmer than I felt. "We can't let whoever is doing this get to us." I couldn't allow that to happen.

As I walked back inside, I could see that

everyone was awake and hanging out in the kitchen. Vance and I exchanged glances before making our way to the group.

"What's wrong? You've got that look on your face." Aunt Thelma stood up from the table and came forward.

"We have some news." I stopped, trying to find the right words. "There's been another murder. Andrew, Brent's friend, has been killed."

"What in the world?" Clemmie's voice rose above the gasps. "Guess that rules him out."

I shook my head. That wasn't the response I was expecting, but Clemmie was right.

"There's also another note," Vance's voice was grim.

"Deputy Jones found it on the front door," I added.

We went on to tell our friends about the message and how I wondered if everything was somehow tied together.

"Let's partner up," I suggested.

"Misty and Luke, you work on tracking down Elizabeth. Find out where she was last night and what she can tell us about Brent."

I look at Vance. "I called off work for the day," he answered my unspoken question.

"Okay, good. We'll head to Harrisville and talk to Honor's sister and see what she knows. The rest of you work on placing wards around our houses and shops. Connie offered to help."

"I'll give her a call right now," Diane replied.

"Anyone have any questions?"

After a round of no's, we all quickly ate our breakfasts and headed out.

I know Misty and I had planned on going to the shop together, but I thought it was smarter for Vance and me to stick together.

Chapter 14

I loved woo shops, as my aunt had lovingly referred to Nicole's store. Witches loved to give mortals a hard time for practicing magic, but in reality, most of us gave them huge credit. The majority of humans had never been exposed to magic, not really, yet they believed in the possibility that something extraordinary could happen to them every day. Believing in the potential was sometimes all that it took.

Vance and I walked through the front door and took in the space. The floors were made of dark, polished wood and creaked slightly underfoot. The air was thick with the scent of burning incense. Calming new age music was piped through the speaker above. As I walked up the center aisle, I looked to the right at all the various crystals. They were arranged alphabetically in neat rows on glass shelves. Their colors sparkled from the sunlight pouring in through the oversized front windows. Glass bowls held the smaller crystals. Little slips of paper were tucked into each bowl, touting the benefits of each crystal. On the opposite wall was a selection of jewelry that I instantly recognized as Honor's. The charms were identical to the ones she sold in her shop. My fingertips instantly reached up to touch the protection charm around my neck. I dropped my hand and moved on. Next to the jewelry were shelves of books arranged alphabetically by subject. I knew that I was a natural-born witch, but I knew I could learn a thing or two from these books. I would have loved to spend time paging through the various paperbacks if we weren't there to ask about Nicole. Speaking of which, I was pretty sure she was working the front counter. The woman in question was explaining to a customer the benefits of reiki when I spotted her. The customer was the only one in the store. I waited until she had finished checking out to approach Nicole.

"Hi, what can I help you with today?" the kind woman asked me.

"Nicole?" I thought it would be best to lead with the name instead of asking if that's who she was.

"That's me. I'm sorry, have we met before?"

"I'm Angelica Nightingale. I live in Silverlake. I was wondering if you've seen your sister lately?"

Nicole froze. I caught her off guard. The

woman stammered, trying to come up with an excuse and failing miserably. I wanted to offer words of encouragement and let her know that I was worried about Honor and just wanted to help her.

But the words never came out because, at that moment, I spotted the mouse I had been hunting for the past day. I didn't even think; I only reacted. As I reached for my tiger's eye pendant and said my incantation, the store seemed to come to life. The crystals on the shelves began to glow, the music grew louder, and the air became thick with the scent of burning incense. Nicole's eyes widened in shock as I transformed into a cat right in front of her.

I didn't give Nicole a chance to react as I chased after the mouse, my claws digging into the dark, polished wood floors as I sprinted through the store. The mouse was quick, but I was quicker, and within seconds I had his little furry body trapped between my teeth. My plan was to transform back into my normal self and take the mouse home for questioning when the mouse shifted before I could. Within seconds I found myself latched onto Honor's ankle. She stared at me in shock. Apparently, no one had told her she wasn't the only witch who could shift in Silverlake.

It was at that moment I realized I'd been mistaken. There was another customer in the store. I didn't see him in the back. He had a pack of tarot cards in one hand and a large smokey quartz in the other. I bet at that moment, he was rethinking his life choices.

"Humba humba humba," the middle-aged man mumbled, unable to form any coherent words. His wire-rimmed glasses slipped down his nose, and still, he stood there babbling.

Nicole didn't hesitate. She whipped out her wand, pointed it at the man, and said the words to erase his memory, "Élaxei."

Vance approached the man as soon as Nicole finished up her spell, planting a more pleasant memory and helping him to forget everything he'd witnessed.

While they cleaned up my mess, I let go of Honor, slipped into the bathroom where I was completely out of sight, and transformed back into my normal self.

"Well, that was exciting," Nicole said after seeing the man out the door.

"Do you want me to lock it?" Vance asked.

"That's probably a good idea," Nicole replied.

Honor still hadn't spoken.

I walked toward Vance and Nicole. "I'm sorry," I said, feeling embarrassed and ashamed of my actions. "I didn't mean to scare you or the customer. I was just trying to catch a mouse that's been stalking me the past two days." I looked at Honor, waiting for her to explain. When she didn't, I added, "We thought you'd been kidnapped. We were really worried about you. What happened?"

My concern seemed to snap her out of it.

"I'm sorry, I wasn't thinking. I wanted to protect myself, but I also wanted to keep you safe," Honor confessed.

"Hang on, what's going on exactly? Last time I saw you, Brent was threatening you."

Honor nodded. "Right, Brent wanted me to create a charm for him, but I refused. You both heard me." Vance and I nodded. "I didn't want anything to do with his plan."

"What was his plan, though?" Vance asked.

"He wanted my help to trap a witch, or more like a sorceress, in a pendant. He'd already conjured her and was keeping her in a bottle like a genie, but it wasn't good enough. He wanted instant access to her power at all times." I looked at Vance. This was crazy. People didn't conjure sorcerers and carry them around in their pockets, or they shouldn't.

Honor pressed on. "I knew Brent wasn't going to give up. That wasn't the first time he'd been in my shop, and he was getting desperate. I was afraid of what he would do next time, so after you two left, I went over to Pauline and asked her what I should do. She agreed that Brent was dangerous and thought I should talk to Sheriff Reynolds about him. I wasn't sure about that, but I agreed because I didn't know what else to do. I was going to talk to the sheriff the next morning when I heard Brent had been murdered. I knew he was involved in a lot of dark magic, and I was worried the killer would come after me next to force me to make the pendant."

"We thought that's what happened," Vance replied.

"I'm sorry, guys," Honor apologized again.

"It's okay. You did what you had to." It was the first time Nicole had spoken up.

"Not to sound selfish, but where do I fit in? Why were you following me?" I was still trying to piece everything together.

"Brent asked me who you were. He wanted to know everything about you. I told him I didn't know much other than your family owned the inn. I honestly didn't know what it was all about, but I was worried that whoever had killed him was going to come after you too, and it turned out I was right."

"Do you know who killed Brent?" Vance asked.

"No, I have no idea. I don't know who started the fire at the inn, either. I didn't see anyone. I only saw the smoke, and that's when I snuck in and woke you up. You'd be amazed at the tiny holes mice can fit into."

"Back up a minute. You said Brent was carrying around a genie in a bottle. Did he have it on him Monday night?"

"He said he did, but I didn't see it. I didn't ask

to. I wanted him to leave. I assume whoever killed him has the bottle."

"Okay, so now we know what Brent wanted you for, and I must say I'm happy you weren't kidnapped." I left off the fact that I was happy she also wasn't the killer. "But we still don't know who did kill him and what he has against me."

"Did Brent ever say anything about an Andrew or a José?" Vance asked.

"No, neither one of those names sound familiar."

"Okay, I promise you we won't tell anyone you're here. If I were you, I'd keep hiding out until we can solve this." I looked at Vance. "Let's call Sheriff Reynolds and see if he knows anything about this genie in a bottle."

"I agree. Something tells me she got out," Vance remarked.

"I think you might be right."

Chapter 15

We made our way through the bustling streets of Village Square, the holiday cheer in the air palpable despite the recent murder. Sheriff Reynolds didn't know anything about a genie bottle. I told him we'd head to the crime scene to see if we'd overlooked it. I left out the rest of the details like how we'd talked to Honor and knew where she was hiding.

The town square was adorned with twinkling lights and decorations, and the giant Christmas tree stood tall in the center. A group of carolers sang festive songs nearby, adding to the holiday ambiance. I couldn't help but notice how everyone seemed to be going about their business as usual. Despite the danger that may still be lurking, everyone seemed determined to enjoy the holiday season and make the most of the time they had with their loved ones. Then again, no one was threatening them. They didn't have a reason to be afraid.

As we approached the tree, I felt a sense of unease. This was the spot where we'd found Brent's body just a few days ago. The Christmas tree was still lit up, the twinkling lights casting a cheerful glow on the scene of the crime, but for me, the festive atmosphere only served to highlight the danger lurking just out of sight.

"It's hard to believe something so terrible happened here," Vance remarked.

"I know. I was just thinking the same thing." I took a deep breath and pushed aside my feelings of dread. "Let's spread out and see if we can find anything."

Vance and I split up. I looked in the back of the tree, and he looked in the front. The undergrowth of the branches made it hard to see very far. I got down on my hands and knees and used the light on my cell phone to get a better look.

"Anything?" Vance asked me.

"No. You?"

"Notta."

I sighed and stood up. "Hopefully, someone didn't find it and take it home." I shuddered to think what would happen if a child had picked it up with the entity still inside. We had to find the bottle.

Vance motioned to the area vendors selling roasted chestnuts and popcorn. I recognized one of them as Amber's boyfriend, Dippy. It must be too cold to sell ice cream. "I'm going to run over and ask those guys if they've seen anything."

"Okay, I'll still look around here."

Vance was gone for a few minutes when I expanded my search area. A few smaller pine trees surrounded the space. When I bent low, my eye caught something glinting under one of the smaller trees. At first, I thought it was an ornament, but the shape wasn't exactly right.

I held the ornate bottle in my hands, examining it closely. The round bottle was made of deep, dark glass and intricately designed with gold filigree. The bottle was about the size of a small vase and seemed quite old with a few small chips and scratches on the surface. I thought this had to be the missing genie bottle, but if it was, the top was missing.

"What did you find?" Vance asked when he rejoined me.

But before I could answer, we were ambushed by an unseen force.

A stunning spell flew right between us; the red streak was undeniable.

I quickly erected a protective bubble. It was one of the charms Luke had taught me the night before, but every time Vance fired off a curse from inside, it popped.

We couldn't tell where the curses were coming

from, but they were relentless. Gold, green, red, and violet streaks shot out at us, one after another.

"Enough of this!" Frustrated and determined, Vance stepped outside of the bubble to face the invisible force head-on.

In an instant, he was hit with a spell, taking it right to the chest. He stumbled backward, his eyes rolling back in his head as he passed out. I ran forward to catch Vance before he hit the ground, but I wasn't quick enough.

Just then, the evil force appeared, revealing itself to be a crazed-looking woman. I had no idea who she was. She had dark black hair that flowed around her head like a halo of fire. Her eyes were a piercing blue, filled with a madness that seemed to dance in the depths of her gaze. Her features were sharp and angular with a body that seemed to be made of smoke and mist. She wore a long, flowing gown adorned with gold and jewels, and it seemed to shimmer and change colors as she moved. She was like a crazed goddess, both beautiful and terrifying at the same time. The woman cackled maniacally as she flew off into the sky.

As I stood there, feeling helpless and alone with an unconscious Vance and an ornate genie bottle in my hand, Craig Daniels, the tavern owner, suddenly ran out to help.

"Do you know who that was?" he shouted, staring up into the sky.

"No. Who?" I looked at Craig from the ground. I sat, cradling Vance's head in my lap. Vance's pulse was strong and steady, but he was unconscious.

"It's Tabitha! You know, the witch who cursed Eleanor?"

I was speechless. Everything was clicking into place, but none of it mattered. Right then, I only cared about helping Vance.

"Here, let me." I hadn't even seen Cassidy arrive. One good thing about being attacked outside Village Square was help was quick to arrive. Cassidy placed her hands on Vance's chest. As she began to chant an incantation, a warm, golden light enveloped his body. I could see the color returning to his face and his chest slowly rising and falling. I let out a sigh of relief as I watched him flutter his eyes open. "Atwhay appenedhay?" he asked groggily.

"What?" I asked, leaning forward.

Vance repeated himself. "Atwhay appenedhay?"

I blinked, trying to make sense of what Vance had said.

Cassidy figured it out. "He asked, 'What happened?' He's speaking pig latin."

"Iyay amyay?" Vance replied.

"Yes, you are," Cassidy replied.

"You were attacked by Tabitha," Craig explained, not bothering to try and figure out Vance's responses.

I hadn't spoken pig latin since I was a kid and it was taking my brain way too long to translate.

"Tabitha? That's owhay ityay asway?" Vance looked over at me.

I repeated the words, translating as I went. "'Tabitha? That's who it was?' Yes, I know. I'm shocked too, but it makes sense. Can you sit up?"

A crowd had formed around us, and I was eager to get out of the open in case Tabitha returned.

"Yeah, I'm okayyay. Ustjay ayay itbay izzyday."

"Yeah, I'm okay. Just a bit dizzy," Cassidy translated before I could.

Craig and I helped Vance to his feet. "C'mon, let me help you to the tavern. You can get a bite to eat, and I'll call the sheriff."

"Thanks," I answered on Vance's behalf. I could tell he was tired and still not fully with it. The language barrier wasn't helping either.

▭

CRAIG AND HIS WIFE, Bonnie, had us loaded up with chili and cornbread in no time. "Eat. You'll feel better," Bonnie insisted. I ignored my bowl and focused on Vance, keeping my eye on him. "You too." Bonnie nudged me.

It took a while to eat anything as friends from around the square kept popping in to see how we were doing. News traveled fast. I knew we had friends, but I didn't realize how much they cared until everything had gone sideways.

Thankfully, Connie showed up, and she recognized Vance's language problem as a tongue-tie curse. She reversed it in seconds. I was thankful for Vance's sake that it hadn't been anything permanent. I couldn't imagine speaking pig latin for the rest of my life.

"Thank you so much. That was a nightmare," Vance confessed, rubbing his head.

"Anytime. I'll catch up with you guys in a bit." Connie rubbed Vance's shoulder and walked away.

"Vance? Thank heavens you're okay," Vance's mom, Heather, swooped into the Tavern, plopped down next to Vance, and wrapped him in a hug. Heather was a level-headed and kind woman, but you didn't mess with her one and only child. "What's this about a ghost witch, and how are we going to take her down?" Heather looked fierce.

"Hang on. I see the sheriff." I hurried out of the booth and walked across the red brick floor to meet him. It would be nice only to have to tell this story once. The rest of the crew knew who Tabitha was and why she'd be after revenge. I remembered when we were trying to break Eleanor's curse and I thought about reaching out to Tabitha's ghost for help, thinking maybe she'd had a change of heart, but Aunt Thelma forbade me from doing so. It turned out she was right. That would've been a horrible idea.

"Sheriff, over here," I greeted him and led him back to our table.

Bonnie reappeared and cleared our bowls. "Anything to drink, Sheriff? Heather?" They both declined. "Let me know if you change your minds."

"Can you stay? I might need your help." Bonnie knew more about Tabitha than I did. After all, it was her relative the evil woman had cursed.

"Sure, whatever you need." Bonnie leaned against the booth.

"What's going on now?" Sheriff Reynolds asked. I scooted over so he could sit on my side of the booth.

"Do you remember a little over a year ago when we freed Eleanor from the tavern?" I asked.

The sheriff grunted. "No, not really."

I looked at Bonnie to take over. "Eleanor's my great, great aunt. Tabitha cursed her back in the eighteen hundreds after Eleanor jilted her son at the altar. It didn't matter that it was for the best; Tabitha refused to let it go."

"And you're the one that broke this curse." The sheriff nodded at me.

"I figured it out, yes." We didn't need to go into the details of how I solved the case and who helped. It was complicated. "I never worried about Tabitha retaliating. Seeing as she was dead, I didn't think we had to worry." I shrugged.

"*Was* being the key word." Vance rubbed his chest where the curse had hit.

"Have you seen her before today?" I asked Bonnie.

"No, not in person, but she looks exactly like her portrait. Elizabeth has it if you want to see it."

"Elizabeth Webb." I shook my head. I shouldn't have been so quick to dismiss the redhead. Brent had been her boyfriend, and now her evil ancestor was back from the dead. Elizabeth had some explaining to do. "Have you talked to her?"

"No, ma'am. Cassidy can't find her either. It's like she disappeared," Sheriff Reynolds remarked.

"That's not good," Heather spoke up.

She could say that again. I brought the sheriff up to speed. When I was done, I said, "As you can see, we need to talk to Elizabeth."

"We're doing everything we can," the sheriff replied.

I wished we could do more. Vance had used a tracing spell to track me down once, but love was the key to making those spells work, and I didn't love Elizabeth, and I didn't know anyone who did. I didn't think a summoning charm would work, either. Those were more for when you lost something like your car keys. I was stumped.

The sheriff's comments brought me out of my

thoughts. "I understand why Tabitha is after you and how Elizabeth is involved, but what does that have to do with Honor?"

"Vance and I talked to Honor —" I started to say.

"You what now?" Sheriff Reynolds interrupted me. "When?"

"A little bit ago."

"Today?"

"Yes."

"Don't you think you should have told me? We've been looking for her." I could see the vein bulging on the side of the sheriff's head.

"Hold on, just a minute," Vance spoke up, his voice sounding stronger than I expected. "Honor is hiding because she's scared."

"Vance is right. Honor is the one that told us Brent conjured Tabitha. He was trying to turn her into a charm. That's why he wanted her help," I filled in.

"Honor was going to come to you Tuesday morning, but when she found out Brent was killed Monday night, she became afraid and went into hiding. She thought the killer would come after her next and force her to make the pendant."

The sheriff took a deep breath through his nose while he thought things through. "Is it possible that this Tabitha killed Brent?"

I looked at Bonnie for confirmation. I wasn't

sure of the extent of Tabitha's abilities. "I suppose she could, but I don't know why she'd go to the trouble of using something physical like a string of lights. You'd think she would have just cursed him to death."

"From listening to you just now, I have to agree with Bonnie," Heather spoke up.

Sheriff Reynolds leaned forward and put his palms on the table. "You're telling me we still have a killer on the loose and a psychotic ghost?"

I swallowed uncomfortably. "That pretty much sums things up."

"You have a plan for how to take the witch down?" Sheriff Reynolds asked me.

"I'm working on it. In the meantime, can you keep trying to track Elizabeth down? She's more important to this case than I initially realized."

"Like I said, we're doing everything we can. The moment I know where she's at, you'll know." There was nothing else I could do but take the sheriff at his word.

Chapter 16

"Hey, Nicole, it's Angelica. Is Honor there?" I called up to Nicole's store, hoping I would catch her before they closed for the evening. The shop closed early be retail standards seeing it was just before five o'clock.

"She is, but she can't come to the phone right now." Nicole's voice was upbeat and chipper, leading me to believe that she had customers in front of her, preventing Honor from transforming and taking the call.

"Okay, listen up. I found the bottle, and I really need her help. Are you guys going to be at the store for a bit longer?"

"No, but let me text you an address. Can I grab your number?" Again, Nicole acted professionally. I knew this conversation would be much different if she were able to talk freely.

I replied with my phone number and waited for

Nicole to send a message. My phone chimed a few seconds later. "That's my address. Can you meet us there in about an hour?" she asked.

"You got it. Thanks."

I filled Vance in on the plan. "I know Honor said she didn't want to help Brent, but I want to know if she knows how to."

"You want to put the genie back in the bottle," Vance surmised.

"Exactly."

I drove back to Harrisville. Vance insisted he was fine, but I could tell he was still sore from the attack. I didn't want him to overdo it. There was no point in telling him to stay home and relax. That wasn't going to happen, and I didn't blame him. I'd be the same way.

Nicole's house was a charming cottage nestled in the heart of Harrisville, not far from her shop. It was painted a warm, inviting yellow with white trim and a red front door.

"Thanks for meeting us here," Nicole said, opening the door for us to enter. "The store was busy, and I couldn't talk."

"I figured it was something like that," I replied. Vance held the door open and followed in after me.

Stepping inside, the living room was decorated with a beautifully adorned Christmas tree, complete with silver and gold ornaments and a string of warm, white lights. A plush, red and white woolen rug lay on the hardwood floor in front of the fireplace, which was dancing with a soothing flame. On the mantle above the fireplace sat several nutcrackers and other festive figurines, adding to the holiday atmosphere of the home. The environment was peaceful. It made me want to cuddle up on the couch with a blanket, a good book, and a cup of hot cocoa.

Honor met us in the kitchen. She'd just finished filling the cream and sugar bowls, and she seemed much more at ease as did Nicole. I wasn't sure what magic Nicole had infused her home with, but the calming energy radiated from the inside out. If I lived here, I'd never want to leave.

I sat down at the kitchen table with a steaming cup of coffee in front of me. Nicole placed a plate of chocolate chip cookies in the center of the table and encouraged us each to grab one.

"Thanks," I replied. "I know it's been a crazy couple of days, but I'm hoping you can help us out some more. I found the bottle." I retrieved the ornate glass from my bag.

"And we met the sorceress," Vance added.

"You did?" Honor's eyes were wide.

"Are you okay?" Nicole asked.

I glanced at Vance. "Mostly."

"I'll be fine." Vance shook his head. I could tell he didn't want this to be about him.

"But we do need your help."

"I don't know." Honor hesitated. The warmth in the room seemed to diminish.

Nicole reached across the table and squeezed her sister's hand.

"Don't second guess yourself. You're extremely talented." Nicole turned toward us. "How did you feel when you walked in?"

I blinked, remembering the sense of peace that washed over me. It permeated the whole house. "I felt calm, peaceful."

"Exactly. Honor did that thirty minutes ago, not even. We were both tired of being stressed out and worrying around the clock, so Honor enchanted the house."

"The energy in here feels nice. I'd love to have something like that at the inn to make people feel right at home," I admitted.

"Stop." Honor shook her head, seemingly unaccustomed to the praise.

"I'm serious." Honor could have a whole side business. Imagine moving into a new house and instantly feeling at ease. You couldn't put a price on peace of mind. I told Honor that.

"You're being too nice," Honor replied.

Nicole spoke up. "You don't give yourself enough credit. You're a strong, smart witch. I know you can help them."

"What is it that you need?" Honor still seemed unsure.

"Do you know how to trap Tabitha back in the bottle?" I asked.

"A bottle? No. A charm? Maybe. I understand how it works in theory, but I've never tried it," Honor confessed. "Despite what you guys think, I don't know if I'm powerful enough."

"How does it work?" Vance asked.

"It's a binding spell. It works best if you have something the person wants. Otherwise, it can be kind of hard to get them to pick up the object."

"You mean she has to be holding the object for the spell to work?" I clarified.

"Right. You get her to pick up the object, and then when she's holding it, you cast the spell," Honor explained.

"Interesting. I wonder if that's how Tabitha bound Eleanor to the tavern?" We never did learn what curse she'd used. We only knew that we had broken it.

"Who?" Nicole asked.

"Sorry, it's why Tabitha is after me. I freed someone she'd cursed years ago." Thinking about Eleanor brought about a revelation. "Wait, that might be it. We might be able to get our hands on the charm she used on Eleanor. It was a family heirloom. Would that work?"

"Does Tabitha want it back?" Nicole asked.

"I assume so. I don't think she'd be able to resist it." As far as I knew, the necklace was Tabitha's.

"Do you think Eleanor kept it?" Vance asked me.

"I don't know, but we can ask her." I then turned my attention to Honor. "If we get this necklace, can you try the binding spell or show me how?"

Honor took a deep breath, seemingly gathering her thoughts. "The spell itself is quite complicated and requires a lot of focus and energy. You have to channel your power into the object, imbuing it with the binding spell, and then as I said, you have to get the target to hold it. It's a delicate process, and if anything goes wrong, the spell can backfire and rebound on the caster."

She looked at us with a mixture of worry and determination in her eyes. "I'm willing to try, but I can't guarantee it will work. The more powerful the witch, the easier it is to cast the spell and the stronger the binding will be."

"No, that's okay. All we can do is try." It was really the only choice we had.

Chapter 17

When we arrived, Aunt Thelma and her boyfriend, Frederick, were at the inn. I'd forgotten he was coming into town.

"You two have had an adventure today. Are you all right?" Aunt Thelma asked.

"We are, and I think I have a plan. Call the gang and see if they can come over. In the meantime, do you know where Eleanor is?"

"Last I saw, she was cleaning the second-floor guest rooms."

"Okay, thank you."

Vance followed me as we walked down the hallway and up to the second floor. It was easy to find Eleanor as she had her housekeeping cart in the hallway in front of the room she was cleaning.

"Eleanor?" I said, popping my head into the room.

The ghost was wearing a pair of headphones, humming to herself while making the bed, and she didn't hear me. It wasn't as if I could tap the ghost on the shoulder to get her attention. Instead, I clapped my hands.

"Hey, Eleanor?" I said with a louder voice.

Eleanor turned around with a start.

"Oh, my good heavens. If I had a heart, it would be in my throat right now. You gave me a fright."

"Sorry, we didn't mean to scare you, but we need your help," I said.

"Oh no, what has Percy done now?" Eleanor pulled her earphones down. "I told him he still owes you an apology."

I hadn't forgotten about the toothpaste-frosted sugar cookie, but I wasn't worried about that now.

Vance and I stepped further into the room as Eleanor set aside her cleaning supplies. Her ghostly form seemed to shimmer in the moon light filtering through the window. She looked at Vance and me with a mixture of curiosity and apprehension.

"No, it's nothing like that. We have some news, and I know you're not going to like it."

Eleanor's eyes narrowed. "What kind of news?"

"I don't know how to say this, but Tabitha's back." I winced.

Eleanor's expression immediately turned to fear. She took a step back and clutched the bedpost for support. "Oh no, that can't be possible," she muttered. "Are you sure?"

I went on to explain how Brent had conjured her, and she was now seeking her revenge.

"She's the one that burned down your bedroom?" Eleanor guessed correctly.

"I'm afraid so, which is why we need your help. We're trying to trap her again." I wanted to send her back to where she came from, but I wasn't sure how to. I'd settle for trapping for now.

Eleanor's hands were shaking. "How?"

"Do you still have the necklace that Elizabeth gave you?" Vance asked.

She looked at Vance, her eyes wide with fear, as he asked about the necklace Elizabeth had given her. "Yes, I do," she replied, her voice barely above a whisper.

"We think that might be the key to making our plan work. Honor says she can try a binding spell on it."

"Binding spell? Like what she did to me?" Eleanor looked at us. Fear rolled off her in waves.

"I think so. There's no guarantee it will work, but we want to try."

Eleanor nodded. "I'll give you the necklace, but please don't ask me to stay and help. Tabitha kept me a prisoner for all those years. I can't risk her doing something horrible to me or, heaven forbid, Percy. I just can't."

"We understand," I said, giving her a reassuring smile, "and we'll do everything in our power to protect you."

"I think you and Percy should get out of the town for a bit," Vance added.

"That's a good idea. Vance is right. You and Percy go. We got this." I sounded calm and confident.

"Are you sure?" I could tell Eleanor wanted to pack right that minute and head out of there, but she wanted to make sure I was really okay with it before bolting.

"Of course, go. I promise. We'll be okay." Now, if I only could keep that promise.

"Thank you," Eleanor said, looking relieved. "I'll go get the necklace for you." She disappeared through the walls, returning moments later with a small, delicate gold chain with a star-shaped locket. It was silver and quarter-sized with a small ruby in the middle

"Here you are," she said, handing it to me. "For everyone's sake, I hope this works.

The weight of the necklace felt heavy in my hand, almost as if it was carrying the weight of Eleanor's hopes and fears. I twirled it around, watching the light catch the silver, creating a shimmering effect. The star locket was delicate and intricate. I closed my hand around the necklace, feeling its energy pulse through my fingers. A sense of determination filled me. This necklace may be small, but it represented so much more. It was a symbol of our hope, our determination, and our commitment to stopping Tabitha and making the town a safe place again.

"Stay safe," Eleanor said, planting a chilly kiss on my cheek before disappearing into the unknown.

I HAD MIXED feelings about returning to Aunt Thelma's apartment. I hadn't stepped foot in my bedroom since escaping the fire Tuesday morning. I knew there wasn't anything left of it, but I couldn't bear to see my childhood bedroom left to ashes. But when I opened the door, I was surprised by what I found. The room was already stripped down to the studs, and half of it was drywalled.

"Frederick's been busy," Aunt Thelma replied.

"I see that," I commented, taking in the transformation of my room.

Aunt Thelma nodded. "He's working around the clock to get the apartment back in shape. He's even hired a crew to help him."

"That's great," I said, feeling a sense of relief wash over me. "Maybe it can be your new office?"

"What would I want one of those for? I don't even like the one downstairs." My aunt laughed.

"This is true. You and offices don't mix."

"I'm thinking of turning it into a reading room. Maybe I'll get a couple of bookshelves, a side table, a comfy lounger."

"Now you're talking." Books were my love language.

I was surprised when Luke knocked on the door with Beatrice and Sabrina in tow. "Sorry, I'm watching the girls for a little bit. I normally wouldn't bring them, but I know this is important."

"No, come on in." I held the door open wide. The twins walked in, hand in hand, and eyed the apartment. "Way cool. This is like a time capsule." I smiled as the girls took in my aunt's vintage decor, which was surprisingly coming back in style.

"Don't worry. We're all ready for the wedding on Saturday," Sabrina proclaimed.

"You are?" At least that made one of us.

"Now, girls, remember, it's all a surprise," my aunt interrupted.

"Oh, that's right. Our lips are sealed." The girls pretended to zip their lips and throw away the key.

"What's the plan?" Sabrina asked. "I heard you're going to take down the crazy witch."

"Yeah, we want in," Beatrice added, warming her hands together as if she was up to no good.

"Absolutely not. My sister would kill me. You guys go sit on the couch while the grownups talk. When we're done, we'll head to the diner for ice cream. How does that sound?"

"Not as much fun as cursing a witch," Sabrina grumbled, answering honestly.

I couldn't help but laugh. Luke shook his head and pointed to the couch.

"Fine, fine. We're going," Beatrice held up her hands in surrender.

Shortly after that, all of our friends arrived. Aunt Thelma poured cups of tea and passed around a plate of cookies while we got down to business.

"What have you got cooking?" Clemmie asked.

"The plan?" I replied.

"Yeah, that's what I'm asking." Clemmie munched on the corner of some shortbread.

I cleared my throat. "We're going to paint targets on our backs."

"Come again?" Clemmie replied.

"We're going to set a trap," Vance clarified.

"Exactly. One Tabitha won't be able to resist." I winked. At least she better not be able to resist it because we didn't have a Plan B.

Chapter 18

As I walked down the aisle, I couldn't help but feel like a walking birthday cake in my 1980's style wedding dress, complete with puffy sleeves and a huge skirt. Eleanor's necklace dangled down my chest like a beacon. I put on a smile, knowing that this over-the-top appearance was all part of the plan to catch Tabitha off guard. Her whole vendetta with Eleanor started over a wedding, and it was going to end with one.

We had spent the past twenty-four hours planning for the elaborate hoax. The inn's patio was the safest place to host the event. Diane, Roger, and Connie worked around the clock to reinforce the wards. Tabitha couldn't enter the inn, and we made sure it was fireproof. Honor was on standby inside, ready to cast the binding spell the moment Tabitha showed up. Honor's sister Nicole was by her side.

Everyone downed Connie's protection potion ahead of time. All we needed was for Tabitha to show up. Every single member of the congregation was packing their wands and ready to fight.

Aunt Thelma had put a heat charm on the deck to keep us warm, but I couldn't help a shiver from running down my spine. I prayed this would work.

Vance was waiting for me at the makeshift altar, looking just as ridiculous in his attire as I did. He wore a baby blue tuxedo that was a little too small for him. A white balloon arch straight out of a nineties prom backdrop was erected behind him. In the summertime, the view from the patio was beautiful, but right now, all the colors were muted and slightly depressing, not at all what I wanted my actual wedding to look like.

The fake ceremony was over the top, from the yards of tulle decorating the patio to the oversized silk floral arrangements. Misty and Daniel even decorated Vance's truck, painting the words 'Just Married' on the back window with streamers and tin cans tied to the bumper.

Clemmie stood beside Vance, acting as the officiant. She wore a black robe like a judge and held a microphone in her hand as if her voice wouldn't carry. We knew Tabitha couldn't be far away.

She cleared her throat and got down to business.

"Dearly beloved, y'all are gathered here today to witness the wedding of Ms. Angelica Nightengale and Mr. Vance Blackwell. Can we say that it's about time?" My friends laughed because it was true, and I knew Clemmie had waited a long time to say that.

Clemmie started preaching, "Love is not just a feeling but an action. It is choosing to put someone else's needs above your own and dedicating yourself to them for better or for worse. That is why today, Angelica and Vance stand before us, ready to make this lifelong commitment to each other."

The crowd was in awe, watching Clemmie as she spoke with passion and conviction. The fake wedding had been arranged as a trap for Tabitha, and as much as I wanted to be nervous, I couldn't help but feel a sense of excitement. Clemmie wasn't a licensed officiant that I was aware of, but maybe she should be.

Clemmie then turned toward us. "Do you, Angelica, take Vance to be your lawfully wedded husband, to have and to hold, in sickness and in health, till death do you part?"

"I do," I replied with a smile. The fake wedding was going according to plan, and now it was just a matter of time before Tabitha made her appearance. I held my breath, waiting for the next move in this dangerous game we were playing.

"And do you, Vance, take Angelica to be your lawfully wedded wife, to have and to hold, in sickness and in health, till death do you part?"

Before Vance could say *I do*, Tabitha appeared,

hovering above us. Her black hair was pulled high in a ponytail. A crown of flames danced above her head. "What is this?" she demanded; her voice filled with rage. "How dare you?"

I took a step forward, standing between her and Vance. "This is what you want, isn't it?" I tried to keep my voice steady. "You wanted a wedding, and we're giving you one."

Tabitha sneered at me. "You think this is funny?" she asked. "You think you can fool me with this little charade?"

"It's not a charade," I replied. "This is a wedding, and you're invited, so why don't you join us?" I could feel the adrenaline pumping through my veins as I prepared for the fight. This was it. This was the moment we had been preparing for. I just hoped we were ready.

Tabitha's eyes narrowed. "I'll join you all right," she said, raising her hand and sending a blast of energy toward us.

Vance and I quickly dodged out of the way, and Misty stepped forward, ready to stun Tabitha, but she was too slow and Tabitha dodged the spell, sending another blast of energy in Misty's direction.

I knew we had to act fast before Tabitha escaped. I lifted the necklace over my head and held it out. "This is what you want, isn't it? Who are you going to trap this time? Another innocent victim?" I taunted the evil witch.

"Innocent? You're not innocent. You've ruined everything! Eleanor should've never been released. She was my prisoner. How dare you!"

Thank goodness for Connie's potion. At that instant, Tabitha charged toward me. Her body pulsed red as her power shot forth from her fingertips. I thought for a second I was a goner as I felt the curses pummel my invisible shield. I held out the necklace, closed my eyes, and said a prayer the potion was powerful enough to withstand the onslaught.

I felt Tabitha snatch the necklace from my grasp.

"Stasti!" Clemmie and Aunt Thelma popped out and shouted in unison. The stunning spell slowed Tabitha down as if she'd been submerged in a vat of honey, but it didn't freeze her. She was much too powerful for that.

"Honor, now!" Nicole yelled. Her sister immediately cast a spell, and a bright light enveloped Tabitha, immobilizing her completely. Vance and I quickly joined in, adding our magic to the spell to keep Tabitha contained. The sphere pulsed with energy as Tabitha fought against our combined power. Tabitha shrieked in rage. The power continued to build and swirl inside the orb. It was then that I realized if she broke free, we'd all be dead. There'd be no stopping her.

Misty, Daniel, Diane, and Roger completed our

circle. They raised their wands in unity, joining magical forces. Tabitha screamed and thrashed against the sphere, but it held strong. We could feel the immense power she was trying to summon, and we had to redouble our efforts to keep her contained.

"Focus!" Connie shouted.

I wasn't sure if she was talking to herself or to us. I couldn't focus any harder if I tried.

The air around us crackled with electricity as Tabitha's curses bounced off the spell's shield. I could feel the sweat beading on my forehead as I put all of my energy into maintaining the spell. My arms shook with the effort. Tabitha was fighting with everything she had, but we were holding strong. It was a battle of will and power, and we were dead set on winning.

Vance and I locked eyes. Together, we pushed even harder. I could feel Tabitha's energy waning, but she still wasn't giving up. Her hatred and rage were palpable, and I could feel it trying to seep into my mind, trying to make me doubt myself. But I refused to let it. I pushed back with all my might.

Finally, the sphere around Tabitha began to shrink.

With a final burst of energy, the sphere disappeared, and Tabitha was encased in the locket dangling from the necklace. The red ruby on the necklace pulsed red and angry. The necklace appeared to float in the air, defying gravity, until it fell to the ground.

My heart was pounding in my chest. I couldn't believe we had actually managed to capture Tabitha. The relief that washed over me was unmistakable. I could feel my knees beginning to shake as the adrenaline drained from my body.

Clemmie was beside herself, her eyes wide as she gazed at the pulsing sphere that held Tabitha captive. "Woo-wee, that was something!" she exclaimed, fanning herself with a hand.

The others were in a similar state of shock, taking deep breaths and exchanging looks of relief. Even Connie seemed stunned by the intense power that had just been unleashed, and she was used to immense power.

I picked the necklace up off the deck and decided to put it in the inn's safe before Sheriff Reynolds arrived. The sheriff was on standby, just waiting for my call. Still, I wasn't taking any chances leaving the necklace out in the open.

"I'll get the champagne!" Aunt Thelma hollered, walking back into the lobby after me. "One bad guy down, one left to go!" she exclaimed.

"Don't remind me." We still hadn't found Elizabeth, and as far as I knew, there weren't any other suspects in Brent's murder.

MY OVERSIZED DRESS swished while I walked into the office and made my way to the safe. As soon as the necklace was secure, I'd change into something more comfortable, and Vance and I would go through a real rehearsal ahead of tomorrow's nuptials. Father George should be here in half an hour. Things were finally falling into place. Sure, we still didn't know who killed Brent, but they weren't a threat to me. They shouldn't be. I had nothing to do with his dark world, and the second this necklace was out of my possession, I'd be safe. If, after the wedding, Sheriff Reynolds still needed my help solving the case, I'd be more than happy to assist, but as Deputy Blackwell. A smile tugged at my lips as I thought of taking on Vance's surname.

As I worked the combination to the safe with my back to the door, I heard the telltale click of a revolver being cocked back. I glanced over my shoulder and stood frozen as Donovan pointed the gun at my chest.

"Hello, Angelica," Donovan said, his voice cold. "I've been looking for you."

I was paralyzed with fear, my heart pounding in my chest as I stood there with my hands raised, staring down the barrel of the gun. A mixture of fear and panic washed over me as I tried to think of a way out of the dangerous situation. My mind raced with thoughts of what might happen next and how I could protect myself. Despite my best efforts to remain calm, my hands were shaking slightly, and I struggled to keep my breathing under control. In that moment, I felt completely helpless and at the mercy of Donovan.

I fought to keep my voice steady. "What do you want?"

"I want what my brother wanted," he growled. "The necklace and the power that comes with it."

"Take it, and let me go." I held my hand out. I didn't want Donovan to take the necklace, but I didn't want to die either. I figured out how to get the necklace back later.

He chuckled, the sound sending shivers down my spine. "I don't think so. You're coming with me. I need leverage, and you're the perfect bargaining chip."

I swallowed hard, trying to think of a way out of this. "Why me?"

"Because, my dear, you're going to help me call forth Tabitha and complete the spell that my brother started."

"Spell?"

"You think he wanted to make a necklace?" Donovan barked a laugh. "No, he wanted to bind Tabitha to his soul. With Elizabeth's blood and your sacrifice, I'm sure it will work." Donovan smiled wickedly and licked his lips like a wild animal, and I knew that's what he was. His face had begun to shift. His eyes narrowed into slits, and his nose elongated into a snout. His mouth widened, revealing razor-sharp teeth and a long pink tongue. The fur on his cheeks and chin grew thicker, and his ears elongated into sharp points. Donovan's human body was a striking contrast to his golden, glowing tiger eyes, which were fixed on me ready to strike. The air around him was thick with the scent of musk and predator. His face was a mixture of anger and hunger, and his eyes reflected a wild, untamed ferocity.

I eyed the gun, remembering Connie's potion wouldn't protect me from bullets. I had to be smart about this. I had no intention of going with Donovan, but I needed to find out where he had Elizabeth. Blood magic was outside of my wheelhouse, but I knew enough to know as a direct descendant of Tabitha, Tabitha's power flowed through Elizabeth's veins just like my aunt's power flowed through mine. Our ancestors were what connected us.

My hand clutching the necklace. I could feel its power humming through my fingers, and I wondered if I could use it to defend myself, but how? I didn't even know how it worked, let alone how to control it.

Suddenly, the door burst open, and Vance and the others charged in. "Angelica, are you okay?" Vance shouted.

"She's fine," Donovan said, his gun still trained on me. "We were just about to step outside."

"She isn't going anywhere," Vance said, his eyes blazing. He stepped in front of me, shielding me from Donovan's line of fire. "Put the gun down. This isn't the way to handle this." But Donovan wasn't listening. He was consumed by his desire for power and revenge. He aimed the gun at Vance, and everything seemed to slow down.

"Who do you think you are? I killed my brother. Do you think I care about you? The idiot thought to challenge me. Now he's dead, and you're next," Donovan snarled.

I saw Vance tense, ready to take a bullet for me, and I knew I had to do something. I clutched the necklace tight, closed my eyes, and focused all my energy on it. I willed it to protect us; to give us the power to defeat Donovan and put an end to this madness.

And suddenly, the necklace pulsed with a brilliant light. As the power from the necklace erupted, I felt a rush of energy coursing through my body. It was as if I'd been plugged into a power source, and every cell in my body was buzzing with energy. My senses were heightened, and I could feel the aura of the room pulsing with the power of the necklace.

A blast of energy shot forth, knocking Donovan off his feet and sending him flying across the room. The gun clattered to the floor.

I had to fight to stay on my feet. The power was that intense. I looked over to see Donovan lying on the floor, motionless. The relief I felt that I was no longer in immediate danger was quickly replaced with a sense of wonder at the power that had just come through me.

I stood there, stunned, as I realized what had just happened. I had used the necklace's power, and it had worked.

I glanced at Vance, who was also dazed but unharmed. Donovan, on the other hand, was starting to come to. He appeared disoriented. He had shifted back to his full human form, and the anger in his eyes was replaced by fear. He looked at me, and I could see the realization in his eyes. He knew that he was no match for me now.

My hand was shaking as I held the necklace, and I could feel the power coursing through it. It was as if the necklace had a life of its own. It was dangerous. Just like the Silverlake Sapphire, the magical gem that protected Silverlake, treasure hunters would come from all over the world to claim this necklace. The sooner it was destroyed, the better.

As Donovan struggled to regain his footing, the door to the office burst open, revealing two young girls with matching mischievous grins. Beatrice and Sabrina, the teenage twins, stood in the doorway, their wands raised high.

"Sorry we're late!" Beatrice shouted, her voice filled with excitement.

"We've got this!" Sabrina added, her eyes shining with a sense of adventure.

The twins shot off a rainbow spell, and in a flash of light, a magnificent unicorn appeared in the room. The beast was a beautiful, shimmering vision of grace and power. It charged towards Donovan, its horn glinting with an inner light.

The unicorn bound Donovan's hands with rainbows, turning his skin pink and covering him in glitter. He struggled against his bindings, snarling in frustration, but the unicorn held him tight, and the girls approached, their wands still glowing with power.

"You'll never get away with this," Donovan growled, his eyes blazing with anger.

"Oh, we already have," Beatrice replied with a saucy wink.

"Besides, who says we want to get away with it?" Sabrina added, her tone playful. "It's much more fun to bask in the glory."

The girls giggled and twirled their wands, sending a burst of confetti raining down upon the room. Donovan was surrounded by glitter, and his once menacing form was now transformed into a comical sight.

I stared in disbelief, amazed at the power the twins possessed and thankful they were on our side.

Chapter 19

"Now we can pop the bubbly!" Aunt Thelma exclaimed as Sheriff Reynolds walked Donovan out in handcuffs. The twins marched behind him, just waiting for him to step out of line so they could blast him once more. Part of me wished he would. I'd love to see what other diabolical spell the girls would come up with.

As it was, they had already hit him with a tickling spell when he tried to backtrack out of his confession of killing Brent. By the time the girls were done, Sheriff Reynolds knew where Donovan had kept Elizabeth. The alpha promised she was unharmed, but he was keeping her locked up in his warehouse in Atlanta. It was the same place he'd planned on taking me. I shuddered at the thought of being held at gunpoint once more.

I needed to let it go.

I was safe.

I took a deep breath.

One thing Donovan was adamant on was he hadn't killed Andrew. The only thing we could figure was Tabitha had killed him. He probably tried to summon her in Brent's garage and it backfired. I wasn't sure we'd ever know the truth. It's not like Tabitha would confess.

Speaking of which, the necklace was currently locked between two magnets in the safe. The magnets would impact the electromagnetic field surrounding the pendant, adding an extra layer of protection, until we could figure out how to destroy it and send Tabitha back to where she belonged. That would be a problem for another day.

I took a deep breath in through my nose and exhaled out my mouth.

The weight of the week was released off my shoulders. We did it. Tabitha was neutralized, Donovan was arrested, and Elizabeth soon would be free. My heart broke for the woman. How many times did she have to pay for her family's sins? Elizabeth deserved happiness, and I prayed that she would find it. I made a note to visit her after the wedding.

"Oh my gosh, the wedding!" I couldn't believe it was really going to happen tomorrow. Unless Aunt Thelma wasn't ready? I really didn't know anything.

My Type A personality came roaring back and I felt the need to do a million things at once.

"Don't worry, everything is ready, and it's going to be perfect," Aunt Thelma reassured me.

I looked up at my aunt. "Are you sure? I don't want to rush you."

Aunt Thelma nodded confidently. "Positive. You'll have a beautiful wedding just like you always dreamed of."

I took a deep breath and willed my aunt's words to be true.

Vance met me and handed me a glass of champagne. "To us and to a bright future together," he said, clinking his glass against mine.

I smiled, feeling my worries melt away as I took a sip of the bubbly liquid. "Thank you. I love you."

"I love you too. More than anything in this world." He wrapped his arm around me, pulling me close.

We stood there for a moment, taking in the chaos around us, but feeling at peace in each other's embrace.

"Tomorrow's the big day," I replied, bumping my hip against his.

"Are you ready for it?" Vance asked.

"Are you kidding me? I'm the one that suggested the courthouse," I joked.

"But you didn't mean it," Vance replied.

"You're right, but to answer your question, yes, I'm ready."

"Good, me too."

The road to the wedding may have had a few bumps along the way, but with Aunt Thelma's reassurance, I was confident tomorrow would be beautiful.

"Hey, you two." Connie approached us. She held a pink shimmering potion in a round bottle. "I was going to save this for tomorrow, but thought you deserved it tonight." She outstretched her hands for me to accept.

"What is it?" Vance asked.

"A soulmate's potion. I was pretty sure it would work for the two of you, but when I saw you work together today to take down Tabitha, I became positive. The potion only works for those who are truly meant to be together," Connie explained. "It will deepen your love and connection and make sure that you never grow apart, or so I'm told."

I took the bottle from her and held it up to the light, watching as the pink liquid shimmered. "It's beautiful. Thank you."

"And if it doesn't work, it at least tastes good." Connie reached out and popped the cork. The smell of strawberries filled the air.

Vance took the bottle from my hands and took a sip. "Strawberry cheesecake?"

"Mm-hmm." Connie rocked back on her heels, impressed with herself.

I copied Vance and did the same. "You're right, this is delicious."

Connie smiled warmly. "It's my pleasure. I just want you both to be happy and have a long, fulfilling life together."

"It's the perfect gift, thank you." I gave Connie a hug, wishing she could experience true love and happiness for herself. Maybe it was still in her cards. Only time would tell.

Aunt Thelma was true to her word and didn't tell us where we were headed until the morning of our wedding. Nothing about our relationship was traditional, and today was no exception. After meeting her at the diner, Aunt Thelma handed us a map.

"X marks the spot," she said with a wink. "We'll see you there in an hour. And don't worry. We'll have everything all ready for you. Now enjoy your breakfast." Aunt Thelma motioned with her arm toward the private table for two set up in the back corner.

Vance's mom, Heather, was waiting for us. "Good morning, you two," she said, handing us each a steaming cup of coffee. "I thought you could use a good meal before the big day."

I sat down at the table, marveling at the spread before me. Heather had topped our plates with stacks of rich French toast, crispy bacon, and fluffy scrambled eggs. There was also a big bowl of fresh fruit and a pitcher of maple syrup.

"This is great, mom," Vance said, digging in.

I agreed, taking a bite of the French toast. It was warm and sweet, with a crispy exterior that was just the right amount of crunchy.

"Leave your plates when you're done. Henry will clean up." Heather motioned to her line cook. "I'll see you both at the wedding." Heather bent down and kissed Vance on his cheek and then did the same to me.

An hour later, I walked hand in hand with Vance down the winding trail that led to our secret wedding location, both of us filled with excitement and nervousness. Aunt Thelma had outdone herself yet again choosing the heart of the forest, a beautiful open meadow at the end of one of our favorite hiking trails, as the venue for our winter wedding.

As we reached the meadow, I was struck speechless. Aunt Thelma had created a winter wonderland. A beautiful arch, draped with evergreen boughs and twinkling lights, stood in the center of the clearing, and rows of benches were set up for our guests, all dressed in their warmest winter gear. The soft sounds of a string quartet playing in the distance added to the magical atmosphere.

Vance was just as stunned as I was, his mouth

agape as he took in the sight. "It's perfect," he whispered, turning to smile at me.

"It is," I agreed, tears of joy welling up in my eyes. "Aunt Thelma has truly outdone herself this time."

My aunt approached us, a huge grin on her face, and led me to a small tent at the edge of the meadow. Inside was a beautiful white gown, trimmed in faux fur, hanging from a rack. "The original dressmaker sent it to me," Aunt Thelma explained. "It's similar to your first dress, but more fitting for an outdoor winter wedding."

"It's beautiful. Everything is."

I was over the moon and quickly changed into the dress, stepping outside and beaming from ear to ear. Vance's eyes lit up when he saw me, and he took my hand, leading me to the arch where Rocky was waiting, standing next to Father George. I hadn't seen the gargoyle since the explosion at the church, but his presence was fitting. Someone had fixed a bowtie around his massive neck. A top hat sat lopsided on his head. Even with his red glowing eyes, the gargoyle looked lovable.

Father George led us through the ceremony. In no time, we were exchanging our vows. Vance went first.

"Angelica, from the moment I saw you, I knew that you were going to be a part of my life forever. Even as life took us on different paths, my love for you never faded, and when fate brought us back together, I knew without a doubt that you were the one I was meant to spend the rest of my life with.

"I promise to love you with all of my heart, to always be there for you, to support you, and to make you laugh. I will be your partner in every sense of the word, and together, we will face any obstacle that comes our way.

"You are my everything, Angelica. I am so grateful to have you in my life, and I cannot wait to spend the rest of my days by your side as your husband. I love you now and forever."

I could feel my heart overflowing with love and happiness. The memories of our childhood, the laughter we shared, and the journey that had brought us back together all came rushing back to me. I felt so incredibly lucky to be standing there in that moment, declaring my love and commitment to the man I loved more than anything in the world.

Tears welled up in my eyes as I looked into Vance's warm and loving gaze, and I knew that he felt the same way. His love for me was written all over his face, and I felt so lucky to have him in my life.

Up until that moment, I wasn't sure what I was going to say. Nothing I wrote ever sounded right, but then and there, the words tumbled out.

"Vance, I can't imagine marrying anyone else but you. You have brought so much joy and laughter into my life, and I am grateful every day that you are by my side. I promise to always stand by you no matter what life throws our way. I will support your dreams and be your rock when you need it. I will love you through the good times and the bad; through sickness and in health. I vow to always be honest, faithful, and true to you for as long as we both shall live. I give you my heart, my soul, and all of my being forever and always."

Saying my vows to Vance felt like a culmination of a lifetime of love and friendship, and I knew that this was only the beginning of our journey together.

As we exchanged rings, surrounded by our loved ones and the beauty of nature, I felt like the luckiest woman in the world. I couldn't wait to spend the rest of my life with Vance as his wife and partner in every sense of the word. The ceremony was magical, and when we shared our first kiss as husband and wife, it felt like nothing else in the world mattered. I knew that our love would only continue to grow stronger with each passing day.

WHAT'S NEXT? **Spellbinding Secrets!**

Stephanie Damore Complete Works

MYSTIC INN MYSTERIES

Witchy Reservations

Eerie Check In

Spooked Solid

Untimely Departure

Midnight at Mystic Inn

Bewitch Break Inn

Potions, Poison, and Pumpkin Spice

Jingle Bells and Wedding Spells

Spellbinding Secrets

. . .

SPIRITED SWEETS MYSTERIES
Bittersweet Betrayal
Decadent Demise
Red Velvet Revenge
Sugared Suspect

WITCH IN TIME
Better Witch Next Time
Play for Time
Time Will Tell

BEAUTY SECRETS SERIES
Makeup & Murder
Kiss & Makeup
Eyeliner & Alibis
Pedicures & Prejudice
Beauty & Bloodshed
Charm & Deception

A DROP DEAD *Famous Cozy Mystery*
Mourning After

About the Author

Stephanie Damore is a USA Today bestselling mystery author known for her fun and fearless stories featuring smart and sassy sleuths. With a soft spot for magic and romance, Damore's books are perfect for readers who enjoy a dash of romance and a twist of whodunit.

For information on new releases and fun giveaways, visit her Facebook group: Paranormal Mystery Coven

www.facebook.com/groups/
paranormalcozymystery/

 twitter.com/stephdamore

instagram.com/steph_damore_author

bookbub.com/profile/stephanie-damore